MW00696556

LAST
TRAIN
FOR MURDER

A totally gripping cozy mystery

TRAUDE AILINGER

Published by The Book Folks

London, 2022

© Traude Ailinger

This book is a work of fiction. Names, characters, businesses, organizations, places and events are either the product of the author's imagination or are used fictitiously. Any resemblance to actual persons, living or dead, events or locales is entirely coincidental. The spelling is British English.

ISBN 978-1-80462-034-2

www.thebookfolks.com

LAST TRAIN FOR MURDER is the third book in a series of amateur sleuth mysteries set in Edinburgh. For details about the other titles, head to the back of this one.

Prologue

She must be dead by now. Her last hours won't have been pleasant, but it really is her own fault. When I think of the time and effort I have put in, and for it all to be ruined by that impertinent, interfering bitch? No way. Investigative journalism, she called it. Obsessed with destroying other people's lives, that's what she was. I tried to make her see sense, but would she listen? Of course not. She never cared who she might hurt, so in fact, I did the world a favour.

Anyway, there is no point in dwelling on the past. The only thing that matters is the future.

Chapter 1

When DI Russell McCord entered the CID department at St Leonard's police station, he knew immediately that something was wrong. An eerie silence enveloped the deserted corridor. The huge, open-plan office, normally buzzing with activity, had clearly been abandoned in a hurry. Files lay open on the desks, and some computer screens had been left unlocked. Jackets and coats were still draped over the backs of chairs, and on one of the desks a half-open packet of crisps had spread its contents over the keyboard.

But surely, DC Heather Sutton would be there. Known to her colleagues as Heather the Hacker for her incomparable computer skills, DC Sutton never strayed far from her screens. Indeed, DI McCord had never once known DC Sutton *not* to be at her desk when he was in, so he made his way to her workstation, which was surrounded by tall filing cabinets to keep out unwelcome visitors, meaning pretty much everybody apart from McCord. He knocked on the outer wall of the defence system, but there was no reply. Tentatively, he went inside, but her space was empty.

Now seriously worried, he walked along the echoing corridor to his office. The place was like a ghost town. Had they all been called out to a major emergency? Surely, he would have been told.

The door of his office was closed. Seized by a sudden dread, he hesitated. Inside, there should be DC Duncan

Calderwood, his loyal sidekick, irritatingly posh and good-looking. What if something had happened to him? Telling himself not to be stupid, he pushed down the handle and scanned his office. Empty.

Determined to find out what was going on, McCord reached the end of the corridor and swung open the door to the large conference room. It was pitch-black and sticky inside, but he sensed a strong presence. His hands felt sweaty, and every muscle in his taut, wiry body tensed in anticipation of an attack. Then suddenly, the lights went on, and a deafening roar erupted as a dozen colleagues cheered underneath a banner saying, 'Welcome back!'

Calderwood came towards him with a big grin on his face, and McCord needed all his inner strength not to punch him. What the hell had the moron been thinking of? Giving him the fright of his life, simply because he had been on leave for a couple of weeks?

McCord only just managed to compose himself and force a smile onto his face, while he was waiting for his heartbeat to return to normal.

Calderwood grabbed his hand and shook it.

"Good to have you back, sir. How was the re-education programme?"

"I am traumatised for life," McCord replied, noticing DC Sutton near the wall, as far away from the others as possible and looking decidedly uncomfortable.

By now McCord was quite moved by this unexpected show of affection.

"Where is Superintendent Gilchrist?" he asked. "He wouldn't like this one little bit."

The Super and the detective shared an intense and entirely mutual dislike. Gilchrist had made McCord take leave after the last, somewhat disastrous investigation and had enrolled him on a programme of courses with the aim to 'examine his subconscious prejudices, in particular his attitude to social diversity and authority'.

If the Super had been out for revenge, he had succeeded: the courses had been more torturous for McCord than scouring the Edinburgh underworld for hardened criminals.

"He is at headquarters today," Calderwood reassured him.

"That's a good start to the week," McCord said. "And now back to work, everybody; and if any of you ever leave your computer screens unsecured again, I'll send you on one of those courses!"

* * *

Back in their office, McCord immediately noticed the azalea that had been a present from journalist and would-be detective Amy Thornton. He had almost killed it by drowning but Calderwood must have nursed it back to health during his absence because it was bursting with delicate pink flowers. He found himself wondering when he would see Amy again.

"Has our inimitable Miss Thornton been in at all while I was away?" McCord asked casually.

"No, not once."

Was he imagining things or did Calderwood sound miffed that Amy hadn't been in to see him?

"Well, judging by past experience, the next murder will send her hurrying into the station," McCord said. "Now tell me what's been happening. How did you get on with the DI who covered for me?"

"She was fine."

McCord grinned. "Of course, she was. No woman can resist your upper-class charm, and even if she could, she would not mess with the son of a High Court judge."

Calderwood rolled his eyes.

"Oh, how I missed your banter, sir. Yes, she was just great. If I'd had a DI like her in Glasgow, I would still be there."

"That reminds me," McCord said, grinning, "there was a guy on the course I was on who used to work with you. Frankie somebody. He remembers you fondly."

Calderwood's handsome face contorted.

"Frank Sinclair," he spat. "He was one of those who made my life a misery there. Whenever there was a call-out, he'd say: 'You'd better let us deal with it. Glasgow is a tough place to work for a pretty posh boy', or something to that effect."

"Well, he commiserated me on having to work with you. I think he used the words 'overprivileged wet rag'."

Seeing Calderwood turn crimson, McCord lifted his hands.

"His words, not mine. If you ask me, he is only jealous, ugly peasant that he is."

Calderwood could not help but smile. "And what did you say?"

"I said that for a pretty posh boy you were shaping up to be quite a decent detective."

While they were working through the slowly diminishing piles of paperwork, Calderwood laughed at some of McCord's anecdotes of the superintendent making his life a misery.

"But," McCord said, "you are still Gilchrist's golden boy, so you have nothing to fear when the next body turns up."

Right on cue, the office telephone rang, and McCord picked up the receiver. After listening intently to the message, he thanked the caller and hung up. He turned to Calderwood, a mixture of excitement and intrigue lighting up his face.

"A body at Waverley, on the Galashiels train," he said. "Let's go."

In a swift, synchronised movement, both men grabbed their coats and made for the door. McCord smiled. It was good to be back.

Chapter 2

Edinburgh's Waverley Station sits in a narrow valley between the medieval Old Town and the eighteenth-century New Town in an area which once held the Nor Loch, a largely stagnant lake renowned at that time for producing foul smells and cholera-inducing bacteria. The waters had been drained centuries ago to accommodate not only the burgeoning railway network and its station, but also Princes Street Gardens. Just to the south-west, perched high on volcanic rock, Edinburgh Castle keeps an eye on the goings-on below.

Waverley Station was fairly quiet now that the main tourist season was over, but a large crowd had already gathered outside the barrier leading to Platform 3, at the eastern end of the station, where the tracks led south, eventually all the way to London and even the West Country and Cornwall. Those passengers with a ticket who had been allowed onto the platform had also managed to get a little closer to the action, but most of the area outside the Borders train had been cordoned off and was guarded by a reticent officer of the British Transport Police. McCord showed his ID and ducked under the tape with Calderwood close behind.

The BTP officer pointed to the nearest carriage of the three-coach train and to the bench opposite where a thin, middle-aged man in a conductor's uniform sat, clutching a mug of tea with trembling fingers. His face was the colour of patina, and McCord deduced correctly that he was the one who had discovered the body.

"DI McCord, DC Calderwood," he introduced himself and his partner. "Could you tell us what happened?"

"It was me who found her," the conductor said, shuddering. "It was awful, the smell, and her face…"

McCord hated these interviews. It always took witnesses ages to come to the point.

"Where did the lady board the train?" McCord asked, trying to focus the man's mind on the facts.

"Back in Galashiels. She was in first class, alone, working on her laptop during the whole journey."

"Did you speak to her at all?"

"Only when I checked her ticket. All she said was 'good afternoon'."

"Did she seem troubled in any way?"

The conductor shook his head.

"No, not particularly. She was tapping away on her laptop, quite the thing. I was thinking, though, that she looked a bit peely-wally."

"Did you see her speak to anybody else?"

"No, but then, I wasn't always there, was I? I had to go through the train checking all the tickets. The journey's not long enough for a trolley service on the train, so there's no other staff apart from me – and of course the driver. I did notice she had water and a snack with her on the train. She probably bought them in Galashiels, but I couldn't swear to–"

"When exactly did you find her?" McCord cut him short.

"With Waverley being the terminus, I always check the whole train once we've arrived in Edinburgh, to make sure everything is ready for the return journey. That includes the toilets, which is where I found her, lying there… I don't think I'll ever be able to forget that sight."

He looked as if he was about to be sick.

"Thank you," McCord said quickly. "If you remember anything else that might help, do let us know."

The conductor nodded, clearly glad to have that over and done with, and went off.

Calderwood sighed as he closed his notebook.

"Not much to go on."

"At least we can rule out suicide, by the sounds of it," McCord said as they boarded the train. "Let's see what Crane has to say."

Dr Cyril Crane, one of Edinburgh's eminent pathologists, was backing out of the toilet in the first carriage and peeling off his gloves when McCord and Calderwood boarded the train.

"Any sign of foul play?" McCord asked.

Crane shrugged, making his exceedingly short neck disappear completely, which, along with his large, round spectacles, made him look more like an owl than his namesake.

"Very interesting," he said cheerfully. "I'll have a better idea after the autopsy. Tomorrow morning at eight thirty. Fancy watching?" he added with a sardonic smile. Other people's squeamishness always seemed to amuse him.

"Towards the end," McCord decided, to Calderwood's obvious relief. "Anything you can tell us now?"

"Female, late fifties, I'd guess, name Martha McGillivray."

Seeing McCord's questioning look, he smiled ruefully.

"No psychic powers yet, I'm afraid. She had a lanyard round her neck, identifying her as a member of the press. Her name rings a bell, somehow; I think she must have been on the telly."

McCord motioned to Calderwood to let their colleagues at St Leonard's know so they could find the next of kin and any other information about the dead woman. From now on, nothing concerning her would remain private.

"Any idea what might have happened to her?" he asked Crane.

"Well, she must have been overcome by sudden nausea and diarrhoea, judging by the state of her clothes. She was curled up on the floor, as much as the cramped space allowed, and her face was distorted in pain. She would have suffered severe spasms and abdominal pain. Could just be a nasty case of food poisoning, but healthy people don't tend to die from it so suddenly."

He reached out to give McCord an evidence bag with a phone covered in brownish, yellowish gunge but it was Calderwood who gingerly picked it up.

"I think we should give that straight to forensics," he said, trying not to gag.

Crane grinned.

"Might be better if you were to come around ten thirty tomorrow morning," he said. "I should have some results by then without harming your delicate constitution."

To McCord's relief, one lucky member of the SOCO team had already squeezed into the toilet cubicle, so he decided to move further along the corridor where a man in a white overall was picking fibres from Martha McGillivray's seat and the area surrounding it, while another was bagging a plastic water bottle and an open packet of crackers. Calderwood leaned forward and took a note of the baker's name.

"Nothing striking yet," the first man told McCord before he even had a chance to ask. "She left her jacket behind with her keys in it, so it looks as if she was in a rush to get to the toilet."

"And her laptop?" McCord asked, remembering the statement of the conductor.

The SOCO shook his head.

"There is nothing else; no laptop, no bag."

McCord turned to Calderwood.

"Right. Get hold of all the CCTV from this station, and from Galashiels and all the stations in between. We need to find whoever took that laptop."

As McCord stepped onto the platform, he was accosted by a tall man whose shiny badge identified him as the stationmaster.

"DI McCord? I was told I'd find you here. Is there any possibility of this train being ready for the 16.25 departure back to Galashiels?"

McCord shook his head regretfully.

"No chance. The train must be isolated to allow forensics to carry out a thorough examination. We have no confirmation yet that a crime has been committed here, but until we know that for sure, we need to preserve potential evidence."

"But it'll soon be the middle of the rush hour! There'll be huge delays! We also need Platform 3 for the service to Galashiels. Could we not uncouple the first carriage where the... where it happened, and use the other ones? Surely–"

"Maybe you are not familiar with procedures at a potential crime scene," McCord interrupted the stationmaster. "We wouldn't want to jeopardise our chances of solving a potential murder just because a few folk might miss their tea, would we?"

"Fine, then." The stationmaster sighed. "We'll send your men with this set to Craigentinny Train Maintenance Depot so they can carry out their investigations. ScotRail will need to provide a driver for that, and they'll have to get a replacement train service organised for the 16.25. Although it might have to be a bus," he said, as an afterthought, shaking his head in despair.

When he had left, McCord turned to Calderwood.

"Let's leave them to play with their train sets. We'll go back to the office and see what they can tell us about the dead woman."

Back on the concourse, McCord and Calderwood had at last shaken off the throng of curious gore hunters when a slim, petite figure in a tight-fitting woollen coat and high leather boots strode purposefully towards them.

"How is she here already?" McCord asked Calderwood with the mixture of exasperation and delight that always accompanied his meetings with Amy Thornton. "Did you call her?"

"No, I didn't," Calderwood said. "It's already all over social media that something is going on here at Waverley."

"Miss Thornton," McCord greeted the journalist with an ironic undertone, "once again, with admirable speed, you have sniffed out where the action is."

"Good to see you back, DI McCord," she said with a broad smile, ignoring his reference to her rather long aquiline nose that she loved to stick into other people's business. "Do you have anything for a hard-up hack in desperate need of a story?"

McCord knew, of course, that he should not share confidential information with a member of the press, but Amy Thornton was not just any member of the press. With her natural instinct for human entanglements and ability to get people to talk, she had helped McCord solve two cases that year, and he knew that even in her hunt for a scoop, she would never let him down.

McCord furtively scanned the surroundings but apart from Calderwood, there was nobody else within earshot.

"Martha McGillivray, in her fifties, journalist, but you didn't hear that from me."

"Of course not," Amy Thornton said, her large brown eyes sparkling with the excitement of an anticipated story for the *Forth Write* magazine where she worked. "You are treating this as a suspicious death I take it? Your Super is going to love this one."

"And why is that?" McCord asked with a sense of impending doom.

"Doesn't it mean anything to you, the name Martha McGillivray?" Amy looked incredulous. "She is, or rather was, one of the most famous journalists Edinburgh has ever had. She covered the London bombings, Salisbury poisoning, even Dunblane all those years ago – wherever there was trouble in the world, in Kosovo or Sudan, she was there. Lately, I suppose because she was getting on a bit, she lived a more sedate life investigating corporate crime and political corruption. Plenty of opportunities to make enemies."

McCord's heart sank. It did not sound as if this investigation would be wrapped up as quickly as he would have liked.

"Damn. Our friendly pathologist, Dr Crane, thought her name sounded familiar, and it appears he was right. Who is she working for now, do you know?"

"Not sure, but I think she has always been freelance. How did she die?"

"It's possible that she just didn't reheat her leftover curry thoroughly enough, but I doubt it. The PM is tomorrow, then we'll have a better idea. Any chance you could find out for us what she may have been investigating?"

"You have no shame, DI McCord, exploiting a poor, needy woman."

"I've never known a woman less needy than you," McCord said. "And anyway, you'll be getting a great story out of this, no doubt."

"Let's hope so. See you tomorrow."

With a wink, she turned away, her neat ponytail swinging behind her. Both men's eyes followed the sensuous movement of her slender body until she disappeared round the corner.

Chapter 3

Back at St Leonard's, there was bad news. Martha McGillivray seemed to have no next of kin in Scotland. Her parents were dead, and she had no siblings or children. The colleagues were now trying to contact a distant cousin who lived in Australia. There was an ex-husband, but McCord decided to wait until there was confirmation of a crime before he approached him.

While Calderwood was allocating the incoming CCTV footage from all the stations between Waverley and Galashiels to different officers, McCord had found an old archive picture of the woman who had died in such a painful and undignified manner in a train lavatory. In the photograph, she was wearing a helmet and a bulletproof vest that made her look rather masculine. She was staring straight at the camera with grey eyes that saw through pretence and guff, and the square, broad chin pointed to determination and even stubbornness. The photographer had caught her anger about the suffering she had witnessed in the tightening of her straight-lipped mouth.

McCord was perplexed by the sudden tenderness he felt towards this strong but seemingly lonely woman. I'll find out what happened to you, he solemnly promised the image before he clicked it away.

McCord started when he looked up and realized PC Surina Dharwan was standing in the door, gorgeous as always. He hoped he had not spoken his thoughts aloud.

"What is it, PC Dharwan?" he asked gruffly.

"Superintendent Gilchrist wants to see you and DC Calderwood in his office," she told him with her film star smile and returned to her duties.

McCord's heart sank. The meetings with Gilchrist invariably left him either furious or deflated.

"I thought he was at headquarters today?" McCord muttered to himself.

"What do you think he wants?" Calderwood asked nervously. "Surely, he doesn't think we have messed up already!"

"No, I bet he wants something nice for a press statement," McCord reassured him. "Just nod and say 'yes, sir'."

* * *

Arthur Gilchrist was in a surprisingly jovial mood.

"Welcome back, DI McCord. How did you find the courses you were on?"

"Illuminating," McCord replied. "They gave me plenty to think about."

Like early retirement or suicide, he thought, but did not say.

"Splendid! I knew they would do you good. And now we're straight back into the thick of things, aren't we? I came over right away from Tulliallan Castle to hear the latest on the Waverley case."

"We're not sure it is a case yet, sir," McCord said. "Hopefully, the post-mortem tomorrow will establish whether it was natural causes or not."

"But you think not?"

"That is Dr Crane's first impression, and he is usually right."

"Quite so."

"And also," Calderwood piped up, "the dead woman is a well-known investigative journalist who apparently has made many enemies, and her laptop has been stolen, probably by the killer."

McCord's dark eyes hurled daggers at Calderwood, but it was too late.

"A journalist?!" Gilchrist's good mood evaporated. "Good God. The papers will be in a frenzy; they'll scream that the freedom of the press is at stake. Killing a journalist is worse than killing a nun these days."

He slumped onto his elevated swivel chair and massaged his temples as if his head was about to explode. Then he looked up again.

"McCord, I think we need to be especially careful how we tackle this one. Any hint of partiality or sloppiness, and we will be crucified. No, *I* will be crucified. After all, it is *me* who will have to face the baying mob. This Miss Thornton of yours, McCord," – Gilchrist waved away the detective's attempt to speak – "must be kept at arm's length. We simply cannot be seen to favour *Forth Write* magazine over all the other papers."

"But, sir," Calderwood almost shouted, "she has been instrumental in solving several cases–"

"But not the Rock Killer case. She didn't help solve that, did she?" Gilchrist demanded.

She did, actually, McCord thought but decided it was wiser to keep quiet.

"And even if Miss Thornton was moderately useful in the past," Gilchrist thundered on, "this time she must get no special treatment, do you hear me, both of you? No cosy chats at the station, nor sharing of any information with her. If she finds out something pertinent to our inquiries, good and well. It is her duty to pass it on anyway. No arguments," he added when Calderwood opened his mouth to protest. "I expressly forbid both of you and anyone in your team to collaborate with Miss Thornton on this case, do you understand me? DI McCord? DC Calderwood?"

"Yes, sir," both muttered through clenched teeth.

"Very well. Surely, Edinburgh CID can do its job without a journalist's meddling. Her easy access to our offices has been bothering me for a while, and now is the right time to put a stop to it. Miss Thornton has to be told to stay away and leave us to get on with our work. Now, I want a daily update on the case, DI McCord, and a clean and swift solution. Get to it!"

And with that, they were dismissed, like schoolboys from the headmaster's office.

A stony silence hung like an impenetrable wall between McCord and Calderwood on their way down the corridor. It would have given McCord considerable satisfaction to rearrange Calderwood's handsome face, but he was preoccupied with the question of how he would tell Amy Thornton that she was no longer welcome at St Leonard's, and worse, no longer involved in the case at all. It would be like telling the inevitable Edinburgh easterly to stop blowing, or the station roof to stop leaking.

McCord sat down at his desk and, still ignoring Calderwood, began scribbling notes on a piece of paper.

Calderwood groaned. "I'm really sorry, sir."

"Never mind," McCord said impatiently. "If that's how Gilchrist felt about Amy being here, then this was going to happen at some point, and he's used this opportunity to exert his authority. We simply have to accept it. God only knows how she's going to take it." McCord summoned all his energy to get up. "Right! Let's go and have a look at Martha McGillivray's flat. We'll take two cars, no point in me driving all the way back to the station and then home again."

Home, for McCord, was a small flat in a less opulent part of Portobello. He took out his car key.

"Hopefully, we'll find an address for a relation in her flat, or even something more interesting. And tomorrow, DC Calderwood, you'll find me her bloody laptop."

It was past five o'clock by the time they arrived in Portobello where Martha McGillivray's spacious but sparsely furnished flat was situated in Pittville Street on the seafront, which is lined with a row of cafés, restaurants and pubs, affording fine views across the Firth of Forth towards the Fife coast. McCord and Calderwood discovered that the apartment overlooked the promenade and the long expanse of sandy beach bordering the Forth. The pools of yellow light emanating from the shoreline streetlights seemed to emphasise the darkness that descends so early in November, rather than relieving it.

One of the keys that had been found in McGillivray's jacket opened the doors to the penthouse. The walls of the living room were lined with bookcases: history, geography, biographies of politicians, phrase books, textbooks and dictionaries for many different languages, but no fiction. On the bottom shelves were boxes containing papers and notes relating to projects she must have been working on. One of them was labelled 'West Middleton'.

"Have you ever heard of a place called West Middleton?" Calderwood shouted to McCord who had gone into the master bedroom.

"No," McCord called back. "Best not to spend too much time on that now. Make a note of the labels and carry the boxes out to your car."

The master bedroom overlooked the tenements hugging the slope leading up to Portobello High Street where every possible space was taken up by parked cars. The few trees in the front gardens had lost their leaves so that they resembled skeletons stretching out their bony arms. McCord pulled the curtains shut. One never knew if there might be a hack from the local or even a national paper lurking outside hoping to get a picture of somebody moving around in a dead woman's bedroom. McCord certainly did not want that kind of publicity, or any other, for that matter. McGillivray had made a half-hearted concession to tidiness by draping her clothes over the back of the only armchair and pulling the quilt over the tangled duvet. McCord searched the wardrobe and drawers, even lifted the mattress. Nothing there gave the slightest indication why she might have been killed.

"She doesn't seem to have had any interests beyond her work," McCord said when he came back into the living room and found Calderwood out of breath from climbing the stairs. "Have you noticed that there isn't a single photograph in the entire flat?"

Calderwood shook his head. "How sad is that."

In the study they searched her desk for a diary, but in vain.

"She'll have had one on her phone or her laptop," McCord said. "Hang on, what have we here?"

In the top drawer of a cupboard, underneath a folder with bank statements and utility bills, there was a thick, expensive-looking envelope. McCord opened it carefully.

"Last will and testament," he read aloud. "Let's see what it says."

After scanning the document, he turned to Calderwood. "We'll need to get in touch with the law firm to verify the contents. There appear to be two main beneficiaries: someone called Zane Smith and a Kirsty Hall. Has either name come up in connection with McGillivray?"

Calderwood shook his head.

"Let's find them and see what their current financial situation is," McCord said. "For some people, a flat on the promenade here in Portobello and a healthy bank account would be plenty motive for murder."

The two detectives spent another fifteen minutes looking for anything which might give them a better understanding of Martha McGillivray, the woman, the journalist and now a corpse. Having found very little to help them, they locked up. Calderwood headed back to the city, while McCord made for home.

Chapter 4

At ten o'clock the next morning, McCord's phone rang. He looked at the display, and his heart sank. He pressed the green button. "What's up?"

"And a very good morning to you, too, DI McCord," Amy Thornton replied, cheerfully. "You are grumpy, and here am I phoning to help you in your investigation into the death of Martha McGillivray. I've been getting some background information for you."

There was no answer from McCord.

"Hello? Is there life at St Leonard's?" she asked.

"Just get on with it," McCord grumbled.

"Oh, we are definitely in a bad mood this morning, aren't we? I don't know if I want to share my information with you after all."

"Please do but be quick about it!" retorted McCord.

"Okay, if you must be miserable! I've found out that Martha McGillivray has worked with the *Edinburgh Messenger* in the past; at least they've had exclusives to a few of her stories. She appears to have been friendly with one of their staff, a Kirsty Hall, who was once her assistant. She might be able to shed some light on what McGillivray was currently working on."

Amy paused, clearly waiting for acknowledgement of her investigative skills, but when none came, she carried on.

"The gossip columns are also buzzing with rumours that McGillivray had a toy boy, a certain Zane Smith, thirty-eight years old, who's been seen out and about with her."

McCord still said nothing.

"You still there, McCord?" Amy asked, now sounding seriously annoyed at his lack of enthusiasm.

"Yes, sorry," he replied hastily. "Thanks, we'll follow up those names straightaway."

"Good. And call me as soon as you have anything from the post-mortem."

McCord hesitated.

"Dr Crane said it could take a while for the toxicology report to come in. Must go, bye."

He hung up.

Calderwood's face fell. "I thought Amy said she was coming in this morning."

"No need to cry," McCord said. "She'll be back before we know it."

"At some point, you'll have to tell her about Gilchrist's order."

"I shall tell her," McCord snapped back. "So far, she has only passed on information to us, as she should. This Zane Smith seems to have been McGillivray's boyfriend as well as one of the main beneficiaries of her will. Find out where he lives. Also, that other name mentioned in the will – Kirsty Hall? According to Amy, she is a journalist at the *Edinburgh Messenger*. We'll speak to her, too."

He noticed the time on the office clock. "Come on, we only have twenty minutes to get over to the mortuary."

* * *

In the office of *Forth Write* magazine a deeply suspicious Amy Thornton put down her phone and turned to John Campbell, her boss, avuncular friend and, she hoped, soon-to-be stepfather.

"Something's up with DI McCord. I have the distinct feeling he's fobbed me off. He was in such a foul mood, he didn't even want to talk to me! He's never been quite so rude before. I really thought he and I had something going. Now I don't know what to think."

John Campbell, immaculately dressed, his salt-and-pepper hair neatly cut as always, shook his head mildly.

"He will be extremely busy with the new case," he said in his plummy accent. "Rumours are spreading that Martha McGillivray's death was suspicious, and tomorrow all the dailies will be clamouring for answers."

"All the more important that we keep up with them," Amy said. "And not only that. We need to find out why she died."

John sighed. "Until we have any concrete facts, I think it is best to start work on an obituary for Saturday's edition; with her CV, there should be plenty of material perhaps even for an extra supplement. In the meantime, I suggest we leave DI McCord and his team to get on with their job."

Amy grudgingly agreed. Rehashing information that was already out there was not exactly exciting, but John didn't have to know that she would continue investigating the case while gathering material for McGillivray's obituary and the possible supplement. After all, she knew that, despite McCord being blind to the obvious, he couldn't do without her. And she had to admit that in the past couple of weeks she had missed the buzz of working on a case, and even McCord's grumpiness.

Zane Smith, the boyfriend, would be beleaguered by both the press and the police, she guessed. But McGillivray's former assistant, Kirsty Hall, could be a useful source of information, and what about the ex-husband McGillivray had shared most of her foreign assignments with?

Amy flicked through her notes and soon came across the name. Shug McCain. He would have many anecdotes to share about the times when McGillivray was at the forefront of reporting on major global events. And the perspective of an ex-husband would be a great deal more interesting than that of a current lover.

After a bit of digging, she found a number for Shug McCain, but when she failed to reach him for two hours, she gave up the direct approach. There was nothing for it; she would have to work her way round from the back, as it were. If you wanted to find out anything about somebody, it was always best to ask the neighbours first.

* * *

McCord had rarely seen Crane so happy.

"It is a real mystery. A welcome change from your usual boring blunt force trauma and stabbings. One might even say, at long last a case I have been *expressly trained for.*"

He giggled as he was putting the remainder of the dissected stomach back into the abdominal cavity before sewing the different layers of skin back together.

Calderwood laughed politely, but McCord just rolled his eyes. "What have you found?"

"Inflamed bowel, haemorrhage in the internal organs, and I'd bet good money that the tox report will show traces of ricinine."

"And in plain English?" McCord asked, barely concealing his irritation.

"Ricin poisoning," Crane said.

Calderwood looked puzzled. "Wasn't ricin the poison used in an umbrella to assassinate that Bulgarian dissident in London, what was his name?"

"Georgi Markov, yes." Crane nodded. "I'm impressed, DC Calderwood. Ricin is not only popular with terrorists and spies around the world, but also with the discerning private poisoner. Even a tiny amount of the stuff kills. The symptoms can resemble other illnesses which is why they are so easily missed by less competent members of the forensic fraternity."

His wrinkled nose indicated that he did not consider himself one of them.

"How does one get hold of ricin?" McCord asked, liking less and less what he was hearing.

"It's so easy, it's frightening," Crane said, beaming. "You buy a *Ricinus communis* – or castor oil plant to those who prefer simplicity. All you have to do is to grind up a few of the seeds and put them in your victim's food."

"No way!" Calderwood exclaimed.

"That is the reason why ricin is called the 'poisoner's poison'," Crane said. "It was hugely popular in the 1950s. One can only guess how many people were prematurely dispatched in those days without the murderers being caught. But," Crane continued, clearly enjoying himself, "to complicate matters slightly, that is not what appears to have happened here because there are no traces of shell in the stomach."

"So, what did happen?" McCord asked through gritted teeth.

His mind kept circling round the fact that he would not be able to tell Amy Thornton anything about this.

"Well, my educated guess is that the poison was extracted from the beans as a colourless, tasteless liquid through a process called chromatography," said Crane.

"Our killer would have to be a chemist, then?" McCord wondered aloud, brightening up at the prospect of narrowing the field of suspects. But once again the pathologist shattered his hopes for an easier search for the killer.

"Not necessarily. A good rummage through Internet and a chemistry set for a couple of hundred pounds should do it."

McCord stared at Crane. "You are having me on, right?"

"Sadly not. Nowadays, though, we can identify the ricinine levels in the blood, urine and serum – if one knows to be on the lookout for them."

McCord sighed. "Can you at least tell us when she was poisoned?"

Crane shook his head regretfully. "We'll have to wait for the analysis but with ricin it is impossible to be precise. It depends on the amount given, the type of bean and the individual it was given to. If I should hazard a guess, I'd say between three and thirty-five hours. We might be able to narrow it down later, but not by much. I know that's not what you want to hear, but it's the best I can do."

McCord groaned.

"Great. You're saying Martha McGillivray could have been poisoned in Edinburgh or in Galashiels, or wherever else she may have been in the past two days. It could have happened yesterday, or the day before, but definitely not on the train."

Crane nodded and neatly cut the end of the suture thread.

"At least you now know it is indeed a homicide, and, thanks to me, you now also know how it was done. Happy hunting, DI McCord."

* * *

On hearing Dr Crane's verdict, Superintendent Gilchrist announced that he was not happy about a murdered journalist on his patch, but his sparkling eyes betrayed the excitement of being able to hold a widely publicised press conference. At precisely twelve noon, as previously announced, he stepped outside St Leonard's police station where a throng of reporters had assembled. From behind the glass door at the main entrance, McCord scanned the crowd but could see no sign of Amy Thornton. No doubt, she would expect him to let her know anything of note. Superintendent

Gilchrist, facing a wall of reporters and photographers, was soon in full flow.

"We are investigating the suspicious death of the well-known journalist Martha McGillivray, who was travelling on a train from Galashiels to Edinburgh Waverley yesterday. I am aware that many of you knew her personally and that you are keen to have as much information as possible. At this moment, however, we are unable to reveal details of the manner of her death, but there will be another public statement in due course. What I can say is that we are looking for a laptop belonging to Ms McGillivray which appears to have been taken from the Galashiels to Edinburgh train. If anyone has any information that might be pertinent to our investigation, they should contact us. Meanwhile, I must ask for your patience while we carry out our inquiries. Thank you."

Chapter 5

After hanging around on the foggy promenade at Portobello outside Martha McGillivray's apartment block for a couple of hours, Amy finally struck gold. A couple who lived next door to the flat which McGillivray had once shared with Shug McCain returned from a pub lunch, keen to talk about their famous neighbour.

Mr and Mrs Bottomley reminded Amy of a couple of plums; both had the faint purple hue of people who like half a bottle of cheap red in the evenings, but Mrs Bottomley was fleshy and round, while her husband resembled a shrivelled prune. Since they had missed the local lunchtime news, they were almost beside themselves with excitement on learning that McGillivray had died under suspicious circumstances. Then, hearing Amy's description of the goings-on at Waverley Station, they were more than happy to reveal juicy details of McGillivray's private life.

"Not that she ever talked much," Mrs Bottomley said disapprovingly, "and he, her husband as he was then, why, he was simply rude. Barely a nod from him when we met on the stairs."

"But really, they didn't need to tell us anything at all because we heard it all for ourselves," Mr Bottomley chimed in. "The rows, late at night, thumping and crashing and splintering – there were times when we thought of calling the police!"

"But I take it you didn't?" Amy asked.

"Well, one doesn't like to interfere," Mrs Bottomley said. "Each to their own."

Amy suspected that their restraint was caused by fear of potential retribution by Shug McCain rather than by an innate sensitivity on their part.

"Each to their own," Mr Bottomley echoed his wife's comment. "But there was one time when it was worse than usual. We heard him shout obscenities and Martha started to scream, and we were worried about her, so we went over and rang the doorbell."

Amy could well imagine how the marital trouble next door had livened up the daily routine of the Bottomleys' dull lives.

"Martha came to the door in her dressing gown, her hair a mess," Mr Bottomley told Amy excitedly. "'Are you okay?' I ask her, and she smiles and says, 'Yes, yes, I'm fine, sorry about the noise, just having a barney over the washing-up.' Of course, I didn't believe a word. But next day she came over with a bunch of flowers and chocolates, apologising for the disturbance, or rather disturbances, because that type of commotion between them went on all the time, really. She wore dark glasses, so I assumed she had a black eye, but she seemed cheerful enough and told us not to worry."

Mrs Bottomley must have caught Amy's sceptical look.

"She knew we were there to help if she needed it, so we left it at that," she said defensively. "And then Shug moved out and suddenly everything went quiet."

"Has she had any other visitors recently?"

"Not that we could see," Mr Bottomley replied, obviously disappointed. "She was out a lot, overnight as well, but we never knew if it was for her job or if she had a fancy man."

"Did you ever see this man visiting her?" Amy asked and showed them a picture of Zane Smith she had downloaded from an old advert.

Both shook their heads.

"Never seen him before," Mrs Bottomley said. "You're not saying that he...?"

Scandalized and titillated at the same time, she examined the picture closely.

"He must be twenty years younger than she is!" she exclaimed with a distinctly jealous undertone.

Mrs Bottomley was probably the same age as McGillivray; yet somehow, Amy simply could not imagine her having a 'fancy man', ever.

"She must have done well out of the separation, or divorce, if she could keep the flat for herself, mustn't she?" Mr Bottomley asked. "Good for her, he is a right brute, that ex-husband of hers."

After a few more anecdotes about McGillivray's marital life, Amy bade the Bottomleys goodbye, more determined than ever to meet Shug McCain.

* * *

Meanwhile, McCord was checking up on PC Mike Turner who was working through the CCTV footage covering Platform 3 at the time the train arrived at Waverley. He had concentrated on the people exiting the first carriage, assuming the killer would have chosen the quickest way out before the body would be discovered. He told McCord that a lot more people exited the first-class carriage than could possibly have sat there. Obviously, passengers must have moved forward through the train in order to be closer to the concourse rather than getting off at the nearest door. What was even more depressing to PC Turner was the number of people alighting who were carrying nondescript laptop cases. To identify them would take days at least.

"There's something I don't get," PC Turner said to McCord. "If it is so difficult to predict when the poison takes effect, the killer could not have known when exactly McGillivray was going to die."

"You're right," McCord said. "If they were after her laptop, they must have followed her around, watching her. Liaise with the colleague who has the footage from Galashiels. We need to find a link between McGillivray and somebody who was on that train."

McCord turned to DC Calderwood who had just joined them. "Let's leave PC Turner to get on with it. Why don't we go and interview McGillivray's toy boy?"

Calderwood did not need to be told twice.

* * *

Five minutes later McCord and Calderwood were negotiating the early afternoon traffic along Gorgie Road in the East End of the city where property prices were more modest than elsewhere and where Zane Smith rented a flat. Fortunately, there was no football match at the stadium of the Heart of Midlothian Football Club that afternoon. A milky sun was struggling through the clouds, so McCord turned down his window a couple of inches, letting in the malty aromas of beer being made at the nearby Caledonian Brewery. He almost expected some remark from Calderwood about the smell, which was powerful and inescapable, but his colleague's thoughts were elsewhere.

"Does Zane Smith know we are coming to see him?" Calderwood asked.

McCord had phoned ahead and been told by Smith in a very subdued voice that any time that day would be convenient. "He may not be expecting us straightaway," McCord said and then added, "What kind of a name is Zane anyway? It does sound as if he's a real prat. Talk about pretentious."

"It actually is his real name," Calderwood said, "and you can hardly blame him for it; if anything, it's his parents' fault."

"True. It doesn't look as if he is holding down a nine-to-five job if he's at home all day. Did you find out what he does?"

"According to his records, he is a model. He was moderately successful in the past, even had a gig with Dolce & Gabbana once, but not much evidence of a career in recent years."

"Maybe he's supplementing his income by befriending women twenty years his senior," McCord thought aloud. "We need to get into McGillivray's phone and emails. Hopefully, forensics will have something for us later this afternoon."

* * *

Zane Smith had not matured well. He must have been very good-looking in a feminine sort of way when he was a young man, but now that the glow of youth had gone and the first signs of middle age were starting to show, he had a distinct whiff of 'past it' about him. His eyes were red and swollen when he opened the door, but he had made the effort to dress in designer jeans and a dark shirt.

"DI McCord and DC Calderwood," McCord said, showing his ID. "We spoke earlier on the phone."

"Of course, please come in."

Smith led the way into the lounge. The furniture was expensive and tasteful but had seen better days. He pointed to the leather sofa.

"Tea? Coffee?"

"Yes, coffee, please, and one for my colleague, as well," replied McCord who always liked to nose around while the host was busy in the kitchen.

When Smith had gone, he exchanged a look with Calderwood and sniffed the air. The stinging smell of raw onion wafted over from the kitchen. McCord pointed to his eyes, indicating that he suspected Smith of artificially creating his tears. He stood up to examine the photographs on the mantlepiece. One of them, taken by a professional, showed a smiling Smith in a dinner suit next to an attractive woman in a satin evening gown. McCord was surprised as he recognised Martha McGillivray. Her smile was a little strained.

"That was on our Mediterranean cruise last summer."

Smith had come in noiselessly and put the tray with coffee and biscuits down. "They always have a formal evening on cruise ships, usually when they have been at sea all day. The guests can get dressed up and have their photo taken before going to dinner. Martha didn't want to at first; she said she felt silly in her gown, but she was so beautiful, I persuaded her to have the picture taken, as evidence, as it were."

He stopped himself at this unfortunate turn of phrase.

"You were close then?" McCord asked.

Smith hesitated a fraction of a second.

"We went out for dinner or drinks. She was not overly keen on the theatre or the cinema. She said the real stories she was researching were a lot more exciting than anything one could make up." He had not touched his coffee. "How did Martha die?" he asked quietly.

"The post-mortem has not been completed yet," McCord said, evading the question. "Do you know what she had been working on recently?"

Smith looked resentful.

"She didn't talk to me about her work. She was a touch paranoid that someone might pinch her story or tip off the people she was investigating."

Or maybe she didn't trust you, McCord thought. "Do you know where Martha went yesterday?"

Smith lowered his head. "She told me she was going down to the Borders, but she didn't say where exactly. I had offered to go with her, but she didn't want that."

"Do you have a job, Mr Smith?" McCord asked suddenly.

Their host's eyes narrowed. "I work as a freelance model."

"Excuse my ignorance, but does that pay well?"

McCord's pretence at innocence was clearly not appreciated.

"It depends on the jobs I get," Smith replied sharply. "It is an unpredictable career."

"Do you know if Martha made a will?" McCord asked.

There was a pause.

"No, but she might have," Smith said eventually. "I once told her to be careful when she was investigating powerful people who had a lot to lose, but she just laughed and said I didn't need to worry; if someone got to her, which she very much doubted, I would be well provided for."

He buried his face in his hands.

"We are sorry for your loss." Calderwood's voice expressed heartfelt sympathy.

"When did you last see her?" persisted McCord, who did not buy the grieving boyfriend routine.

"The day before yesterday," Smith said without hesitation. "We went to the SKYbar for drinks." His eyes filled with tears. "We met a friend of Martha's, a journalist as well. She was there with the mother of her partner to celebrate her expecting a baby. We briefly stopped at their table to have a toast."

"Do you happen to know the name of that journalist?" McCord asked.

"Kirsty somebody. Martha said she used to be her assistant, but I had never met her until the day before yesterday."

"How did Martha seem to you then? Was she on good form?" McCord asked.

"She was her usual self," Smith said wistfully. "I gave her a row for downing a glass of champagne before the hostess had even returned to the table. But as always, she just laughed at me."

It seemed Smith was about to say something else but decided against it.

McCord drained his cup and stood up.

"Thank you very much, Mr Smith. I think that's all for now. We may have to speak to you again, so please don't leave the city in the meantime without telling us. We'd be grateful if you could write an account of your whereabouts during yesterday and the day before and drop it off at St Leonard's police station as soon as it is convenient."

Smith jumped out of his armchair.

"So, you think that somebody killed her? And that it was *me*?"

"Not at all," McCord said, unconvincingly. "We ask everybody connected to an inquiry for their alibi. It helps us to eliminate people and saves a lot of time and effort."

"It will be a very short account. I was at home most of the time," Smith said bitterly. "Why don't you ask that ex-husband of hers? He's a violent drunkard and treated Martha so appallingly that she never wanted to commit to a relationship again."

He turned to Calderwood.

"Can you tell me at least that she didn't suffer?"

Calderwood shook his head regretfully. "We're still waiting for the results of the post-mortem. I'm sorry."

Smith said nothing more as he showed them out.

Chapter 6

Back at the station, Calderwood was sticking a photo of Zane Smith on the incident board.

"I don't know why you were so hard on him," he said to McCord. "I had the impression that he was genuinely grieving."

McCord shrugged.

"He's a sponger. Who do you think paid for that cruise? And that photo; maybe it wasn't the dress that made her unhappy – why would it be? She looked great in it. I suspect it was because their relationship had turned sour. I'll never understand why she took up with a guy like that in the first place. A model, for God's sake!"

"But even if he *was* a sponger, why would he kill her? He'd lose everything. If she paid for their drinks and meals, and even a cruise?" Calderwood argued.

"Maybe that was not enough anymore. Come on, it's time to speak to the people at the *Edinburgh Messenger*, especially this other journalist, Kirsty Hall."

* * *

Dougal Johnstone, the editor of the *Edinburgh Messenger*, had the hungry demeanour of a real hack and was keen to assist the police in their inquiries, no doubt hoping for some useful information in return.

"I can't believe Martha is dead. She was so..." – he made a show of trying to find the right word – "vibrant.

How did she die? All the press announcement said was that her death was suspicious."

"And that is all we know at the moment. I dare say you will find out along with the rest of us what exactly happened. Can you tell me what she was working on?" McCord asked.

"Clearly you have no idea how Martha operated," Johnstone said. "She never revealed anything about her investigations until she had a story well and truly in the bag. You do realise that she wasn't on our payroll? She didn't really work for us at all; she was freelance. She used to cover all the hotspots, you know, the first Gulf War, Kosovo, Darfur, the tsunami in 1994 – you name it, she was in the thick of it. Lately, she stayed closer to home investigating corruption in politics and business. She usually offered me the stories first because she knew we were not afraid of a bit of controversy and would never water down a story to keep local politicians sweet. It wasn't the money she was after; she just loved bringing a powerful bad guy down."

"Was she close to any of your colleagues here?"

Johnstone nodded.

"You might want to talk to Kirsty, Kirsty Hall. She used to be Martha's assistant before joining us. Kirsty!" he shouted across the room. "Come over here a minute!"

A tall, blonde woman hurried across the floor but stopped suddenly when she recognised the detectives. Then she seemed to realise that her hesitancy made her appear suspicious and came smartly forward, holding out her hand, first to McCord and then Calderwood.

"I recognise you from the Rock Killer case. That was quite a long-running story," she said, her pale face lighting up.

"Not my finest moment," McCord said. "But we're here to ask you a few questions about Martha McGillivray."

Kirsty Hall hung her head, so her thick, honey-coloured braids covered her face. "I still can't take it in. What happened to her?"

"We're not sure yet. Could you tell us what your relationship with Martha McGillivray was?" McCord asked gently.

Hall lifted her head.

"We worked quite closely together when I was her assistant. I was on a work experience programme when we got chatting at a press conference, and afterwards she asked if I was interested in working for her. Was I interested? The woman was a legend!"

McCord nodded sympathetically.

"So, what made you stop working for her?" Calderwood butted in.

"I grew out of the job," Hall said, looking surprised at the edge in Calderwood's voice. "Martha felt it was time for me to stand on my own two feet and find a job as a reporter. We kept in touch, shared thoughts on current affairs and sometimes went out for a coffee or a drink to catch up."

"What was she working on?"

"No idea," Hall said. "Martha was quite... proprietorial about her stories."

Interesting, McCord thought. Smith had said the same thing, so at least that seemed to be true.

"When did you see her last?" Calderwood asked.

"The day before yesterday, the day before she died. We met by chance at the SKYbar. I was there with my partner's mother to celebrate my news" – she patted her still invisible bump – "and Martha came in with this guy she had been seeing for the past few months or so. He's called Zane. I don't know his surname, Martha never mentioned it," she said dismissively.

"I have the impression that you did not approve of this Zane fellow?" McCord said, taking charge of the interview again.

Hall shrugged.

"It was not my place to approve or disapprove of him. It was her life, her decision." There was a pause. "They just didn't seem terribly well suited."

She was clearly reluctant to say more, and McCord did not press her.

"Can you think of anybody who would have wanted to hurt Martha?" he asked instead.

Hall gave a derisory snort.

"Take your pick. Wherever she went, careers and reputations were destroyed. Quite a few of her targets ended up in prison."

"Where did Martha keep her notes, I mean, all the information she might have on the people she either investigated in the past or currently?" McCord asked.

Hall thought about that for a moment.

"On her laptop. She also kept some paper files at home, but most of it was on her computer. I heard on the news it was missing. Have you found it yet?"

"No, but the search continues," McCord said.

Hall's face showed a mixture of disbelief and curiosity.

"You think she was killed because of her laptop?" she asked.

Then she nodded, smiling.

"Good luck to them trying to get into her files; Martha had all the protection there is on that machine. But then again, maybe someone simply wanted to destroy any information she might have gathered on them."

"Well, that's a possibility we'll need to consider, but thanks for your help." McCord gave her his card. "I think that is all for now but if you can think of anything else that might help, please give me a call."

Hall twisted the card in her hand.

"Will do," she said.

* * *

Back at the station late afternoon, McCord went over to PC Dharwan, who was still sifting through the many boxes they had brought from McGillivray's flat.

"Found anything interesting yet?"

As well as looking like a Bollywood star, PC Dharwan was one of CID's most promising officers and had proved to be a reliable ally to McCord in the McAdie case.

"Most of what's in here are old stories that McGillivray had already published, but this particular one is still ongoing."

She pointed to the box labelled 'West Middleton'.

"Where the hell is West Middleton?" asked McCord. "I've never heard of it."

"That's because it doesn't exist – yet. It is a new commuter town planned for the area west of Gorebridge, a three-hundred-million-pound project. Infrastructure, shops, hundreds of residential buildings, a school etc."

McCord whistled through his teeth.

"That would be worth killing for," he said. "So, what's the story?"

"The contract was put out to tender, and an Edinburgh company was in the running for it, but then the contract was unexpectedly awarded to Lomax Construction. There is a letter here from the Edinburgh company suggesting that McGillivray investigate the owner, Godfrey Lomax, because they were sure that the whole thing was rigged. Lomax Construction have their headquarters in Galashiels, and maybe money changed hands between Godfrey Lomax and someone on the council's planning committee."

"That would tie in with McGillivray's trip to Galashiels on the day she died," McCord thought aloud. "I bet she paid a visit to this Godfrey Lomax."

"There is more." Dharwan shuffled some papers on another pile. "The locals are not enamoured with the project, either. There have been bad-tempered meetings in the surrounding village halls, various petitions and reports of some verbal attacks on the members of the planning committee. Existing businesses in Gorebridge fear the increased competition and claim that such a huge project would damage tourism, and then there are, of course, the environmentalists who are concerned about the impact on the wildlife in the area and the loss of recreational space."

"That is always the case with such projects, though, isn't it?" McCord argued. "Nobody wants a massive building site in their backyard. Aren't they called NIMBYs?"

"Sure, but there are also rumours that the Environmental Impact Assessment was doctored. It seems that McGillivray managed to get a copy of that, and there are lots of clippings from the local newspaper and even minutes from council meetings. But I can't see any evidence in McGillivray's notes of Lomax breaking the law."

"We need to find McGillivray's laptop," McCord said. "I bet all the sensitive stuff is on that. Good work, though, Dharwan."

He picked up the sheets of paper she had left out for him and moved on to DC Sutton's workstation. Cautiously, he knocked on the outer wall.

"Come in," a hoarse voice called.

DC Sutton spoke so rarely that her vocal cords needed to warm up first when she did. McCord had learned from previous encounters to avoid metaphorical language and to keep it brief.

"Find out what you can about Godfrey Lomax and his construction company before I go to Galashiels tomorrow. Anything on the members of the planning committee for that area, too, especially if anybody on the committee is in financial difficulties."

Since the research she had done for him in the past had often been, to put it mildly, borderline illegal, he thought it wise to add, "All strictly within the rules, of course. Thank you."

DC Sutton took the sheets without taking her eyes off the screen and nodded. McCord smiled and left. If there was anything dodgy to be found at Lomax Construction, DC Sutton would find it.

Chapter 7

While he was working his way through the open-plan office to learn if anything of note had cropped up, McCord checked on PC Turner who was going through the CCTV from Galashiels station.

"Any luck so far?"

The young constable looked up from the split screen showing different stations and swivelled around in his chair.

"There are quite a few people, including McGillivray, who got on the train carrying laptop bags. I'm trying to figure out where they all left the train. There must be somebody who got on without one and came off at Waverley with McGillivray's bag."

"Good thinking, PC Turner, keep at it."

McCord saw Calderwood waving from the door, miming a phone call, and sprinted back to his office.

"Ricinine in the serum; 23ng/mL, and a similar amount in the urine," Crane announced without preamble.

McCord sighed. "And what does that mean for my investigation?"

"It means that it is certain that Martha McGillivray was murdered by ricin poisoning, most likely administered to her food or drink, between three and thirty-five hours before she died, depending on the dose she received, and there is no way to tell what that was. The seeds vary in their ricin content, and it depends on the method of extraction, too. I'm afraid I can't be more precise, but the post-mortem does confirm what I suspected had been the cause of death."

McCord groaned. Twenty-seven hours of tracing back every meal.

"Okay, thanks, Dr Crane." He put the receiver down.

"Was that the result of the PM?" Amy's voice rang out as she stepped into the office.

McCord almost jumped out of his chair.

"How did *you* get in here?" he demanded.

"Through the door, as always," Amy snapped. "I've got something for you. Hello, Duncan."

Calderwood shot up and pulled over a chair for her, while McCord was wriggling in his. What was Calderwood thinking of, inviting her to sit? He tried to remember if the Super was in the building today. Either way, he had to get Amy out of here, but first he wanted to hear if she had found out anything to help them.

"Hello? Earth calling!" Amy turned to McCord. "What *is* the matter with you? You've been acting so strange recently; I mean, you always were rude and ungrateful, but this is taking it to another level!"

McCord avoided her gaze.

"Sorry, a lot on my mind. It's just been confirmed that Martha McGillivray was murdered."

"Well, that's not exactly a surprise, is it?" Amy said. "Anything more specific?"

"Not yet," he lied. "What have you got?"

McCord winced as Amy triumphantly settled down in front of his desk.

"McGillivray's ex, Shug McCain, seems to have been a real brute. According to the neighbours, there were frequent fights and crockery getting smashed during the time McGillivray and McCain shared the flat. Once the neighbours went over to ask them to pipe down, but when Shug opened the door, drunk and in underpants, waving an empty bottle, they fled in horror."

"Hm," mumbled McCord, "we don't have him on the system."

"Apparently, nothing was ever reported to the police. McGillivray spoke to the neighbours afterwards in the hall and made light of it. On another occasion, she even bought them flowers and chocolates to apologise for the noise."

"McGillivray clearly didn't want any negative publicity directed at her," McCord said. "But what could be his motive for killing her?"

"Well," Amy said, beaming, "when they separated, in October last year, she kept the nice flat in Portobello. He is renting a room in Dalry. He can't be happy with the outcome. Had they actually been divorced yet? Maybe they were still fighting over the spoils? After all, most divorces end in acrimony and ill feeling, don't they?"

"I suppose so." McCord fell silent.

Amy gave him the familiar despairing look indicating that she, yet again, might have to investigate this promising angle herself.

"So, what did Dr Crane have to say about cause and time of death?" Amy persisted.

McCord's face was inscrutable.

"What is it, McCord? Spit it out!"

He got up and stood by the window, gazing out onto St Leonard's Street. It was one of those Edinburgh November days that never seemed to reach any brightness beyond a depressing twilight.

"Superintendent Gilchrist has given specific orders that there is to be no cooperation between us, I mean, between you and the station, including Calderwood, and no preferential treatment, meaning all the press outlets are to get the same prepared statements, which means you can't just walk in here anymore, and we can't meet outside the station either."

Amy had never heard McCord use such a convoluted sentence before and took a while to process what he had been trying to say.

"You are *throwing* me *out*?"

McCord lifted his hands defensively. "Not me, Gilchrist is."

"Believe me, we tried," Calderwood said, but Amy ignored him.

She rose, her back as straight as a rod.

"Well, then I shall go."

At the door she turned back and looked both detectives up and down.

"*Preferential treatment*? Pah! We'll see how far you get without me!"

And with a furious swing of her ponytail, she disappeared down the corridor.

McCord banged his fist so hard on the window that the pane threatened to crack.

"Why is she blaming *me*? Why is she always so damn *unreasonable*? And what makes her think we can't solve a case without her constant interference? Who does she think she is?!"

Calderwood wisely refrained from making any comment.

* * *

As she was leaving the building, Amy fought back tears of fury and contemplated all kinds of pain she would like to inflict on DI McCord but decided instead that the best and most sensible solution was for her to solve the case before him and make him beg for her help. That would hurt him even more. Just you wait, DI McCord, she thought, just you wait.

* * *

McCord and Calderwood had not spoken for a while. McCord pretended to be immersed in the study of the case while Calderwood sat there idly, looking miserable.

McCord, in contrast, was simply furious at the injustice of it all. He was mad at Gilchrist, mad at Amy and, for a reason he could not quite figure out, mad at Calderwood as well. As if to torment him further, his phone rang.

"Yes?!" he barked into it.

The person at the other end hesitated.

"Eh, DI McCord? Dougal Johnstone here, editor of the *Edinburgh Messenger*."

"Oh, yes?" McCord's voice softened. "Have you remembered anything else about Martha McGillivray?"

"No, but we've just had an interesting phone call. Anonymous. The caller claims to have Martha's laptop. He is demanding two thousand pounds in cash in a plastic bag to be dropped off at a location he is going to disclose nearer the time. No police, he said, or the deal is off, and he'll destroy the laptop. But I thought, this is a murder inquiry, and he could be Martha's killer, so I decided to phone you."

"You've done the right thing, Mr Johnstone," McCord said, his mood lifting considerably. "We'll send someone round to put a tap on your phone, so we can get a recording of his voice and find out immediately what his demands are. When he calls again, agree to it in principle but try to delay."

"What about the money?"

"We're not supposed to give out ransom money," McCord said. "Cut up some paper in the right shape for the bank notes and wrap it in cling film so that it is difficult to make out, and then put it in a plastic bag."

"But what if he notices that the money is fake and turns on me?" Johnstone asked. "He could be a killer!"

"We have no proof that he is. It might simply have been an opportunistic theft. If he had killed for the laptop, it would be worth considerably more to him than two thousand quid. Anyway, my men will be there to protect you. I'll give you my mobile number. Call me immediately if you hear anything."

* * *

Superintendent Gilchrist was even more excited than McCord.

"Splendid," he repeated, rubbing his hands. "We catch the man at the handover, and either he is the killer, or he will lead us to him."

"I'm not so sure about that," McCord said, pouring cold water on Gilchrist's enthusiasm. "I doubt that someone would go to the bother of poisoning Martha McGillivray in advance, follow her onto the train and steal her laptop only to flog it off a few days later for a couple of thousand quid. But still," he added quickly, seeing Gilchrist's face cloud over, "catching the thief and getting our hands on the laptop would be a huge step forward. We think the laptop may hold evidence as to why she was killed."

"Fine," Gilchrist said, more soberly. "Get the handover set up and keep me posted."

* * *

McCord leaned back in his chair and rubbed his throbbing temples. After preparing the handover as far as they could at this stage, he had sent Calderwood home. At the beginning of each case, McCord always felt he should stay until they had achieved some kind of breakthrough. Maybe the handover of the laptop would prove to be it. Yet, he could not shake off the feeling that this was not a case that would be wrapped up quickly. There was no tangible evidence, but they had a host of suspects. His mind was swirling, and he knew he needed to get away, put some distance between himself and the case and just be plain Russell McCord for a little while.

A late November evening was not the time for birdwatching, so the next best thing was a beer and a curry with his dad. McCord worried about him, being lonely and getting old. I must try to see him more often, he thought as he pressed the speed dial on his phone.

"Dad? Is it too late for a curry and a game of chess tonight?"

There was the slightest hesitation at the other end, which was a little unusual. His dad had always jumped at the idea of a curry night.

"Are you okay, Dad?" he asked.

After being reassured that everything was fine and told to get a lamb pasanda with a garlic naan, McCord left for his childhood home in Niddrie.

* * *

His father had left the door ajar. McCord, carrying the bag with the dinner in one hand and a four-pack of beer in the other, pushed it open with his shoulder.

"Hi, Dad!" he shouted.

Keith McCord rushed out from the kitchen where the plates were heating up in the ancient oven.

"Good to see you, son," he beamed, affectionately squeezing McCord's shoulder as he always did. Hugging was not something they had ever done.

"Everything okay, Dad?" McCord asked again, eyeing him closely.

In fact, if anything, his father looked better than he had done in a long time. There was something fresh and bouncy about him that struck McCord as odd. He even caught the unmistakable whiff of aftershave when he stood close to his dad in the kitchen, putting the bag on the Formica table and the beer in the fridge.

"I prefer the garlic naan to the Peshwari," Keith McCord said.

They had shared a take-away at least once a week ever since McCord could remember, and McCord knew all his father's preferences on the menu. What was the matter with him? He seemed edgy.

They piled the food high on the hot plates, lifted a can of John Smith's that was always sitting ready in the fridge, and took their dinner through to the living room. McCord furtively scanned the room for any changes, any hint of something not quite right. Everything seemed in its place. His mother, photographed not long before she had died giving birth to him, was smiling down on them from the mantelpiece, and the tacky little souvenirs from trips his dad had made lined the windowsills as always. The only new addition was a silver cup on the sideboard.

"What is this?" he asked, picking it up.

"Remember, I won the men's bowling competition three months ago," Keith reminded his son.

"Of course," McCord said. "Why did it take so long to get the trophy to you?"

"Oh, it came soon afterwards but I couldn't be bothered unpacking it and putting it up until now."

"Right," McCord said slowly. His dad was definitely not himself.

"Never mind," Keith said cheerfully, "I reckon you have other things on your mind."

"True."

"How is the case going anyway?" Keith asked.

"Not great," McCord admitted, "but it's early days. Plenty of leads. Most of them probably getting us nowhere, but we just have to keep working at it."

Keith smiled. "Sorry, you probably came here to forget about it all for a little while."

McCord nodded and tore a bit off his naan. His dad was oddly cheerful tonight, yet cagey at the same time. What was going on? But his brain bluntly refused to work on any more mysteries, so he took a large gulp of beer instead. He had a terrible feeling that his dad would destroy him at chess tonight, and, as it turned out, he was right.

Chapter 8

It had only taken Amy a few minutes on the phone to persuade Kirsty Hall to join her for a coffee and a chat the following day at Caffe Centro, not far along the street from the offices of *Forth Write* magazine. Hall had read Amy's serialised features on the McAdie and the Rock Killer cases, and the general perception that Amy was closely working with DI McCord had been very much in her favour. After all, Hall was a journalist and would only be interested in people who she thought were in the know.

"I've always been such a fan of Martha and her work," Amy gushed as they sat down at a table by the window. "I was actually about to write a feature about her in *Forth Write* magazine when all this happened. We may put a supplement into the weekend edition."

Hall nodded. "Martha was certainly a one-off. She seemed to have a sixth sense where a good story was to be found. We will miss her."

Hall pulled out a tissue, but Amy noticed that she did not use it in the end. "I still can't take it in. I just wish I knew what happened to her. The mere thought that she might have suffered..."

Hall stirred her latte, waiting for Amy to comment.

"The post-mortem report is not finalised yet," Amy lied blithely. As much as she resented what she considered to be McCord's treachery of her at this moment, she would never betray his confidence. "But for what it's worth, I think she was murdered, and by somebody who wanted to shut her up. We have to help find the killer, because who knows which one of us will be next? And while the police have their ways, they're snowed under with work. And then there are endless rules and regulations. The paperwork is colossal, or so I'm told. I do think they need our help."

Hall nodded thoughtfully.

"You might be right. But I'm not convinced that the motive for Martha's murder lies with one of her investigations. Maybe it is more personal than that."

"Ah? Are you thinking of the boyfriend, Zane Smith, or the ex-husband?" Amy asked.

"It's possible," Hall said. "Martha tended to evoke very strong feelings in whoever she became close to." She quickly scanned the room to see if anybody might be in earshot, then lowered her voice. "But I was thinking more along the lines of a colleague of mine at the paper, a guy called Cameron Coates."

"Really?" Amy put down her cup. "What did he have against Martha?"

"He's been working for the *Messenger* for at least ten years and still hasn't got a promotion. He is only an average guy, but he fancies himself as the next chief political correspondent for Reuters. He blamed Martha for his stalled career and accused our boss of giving her preferential treatment. He said this to her face in front of us all in the office!"

"And did he have a point?" Amy asked.

Hall snorted derisively. "The simple truth is that Martha always had the best stories, and they were worth every penny the paper paid for them. He's simply not in the same league as her."

Amy was intrigued, but still sceptical.

"Do you really think that he would kill her out of jealousy?"

Hall shrugged. "I don't know. Martha once showed me nasty messages he had sent her, some of them threatening. I told her to report him to the boss or the HR department, but she just laughed and said Cameron was nothing but a pathetic little loser."

"As her friend, did you not report those threats to the police?"

Hall shook her head and frowned. Amy realised she had made a mistake. If she was really as close to McCord as she had claimed, she would have known the answer to that.

"It would have been a pretty serious accusation, so I didn't say anything. To be honest, I was also worried that Cameron would find out and make my life hell at work. Even if he is not a killer, I don't want him to have me in his sights."

Amy nodded sympathetically. "Maybe we can find out discreetly where he was around the time of the murder."

With a bit of luck, Hall would interpret the 'we' as Amy and the police, but Amy hoped that Hall might shed some light on the matter herself.

"I've been asking around casually," Hall said. "That day, he was out and about to do some research and a couple of interviews, so depending on the time of death, he might not have an alibi."

Amy felt a wave of anger at McCord. If he hadn't been so obnoxious, she would have passed that information on, and DC Sutton could have followed the trail left by Cameron Coates' credit card purchases during the period in question. But McCord never took her ideas seriously, anyway, so there was no point. Sadly, *Forth Write* magazine did not have an employee with DC Sutton's IT skills.

"...between you and that detective?" Hall was eyeing her curiously.

Amy had missed the first part of the question but filled in the gap correctly. She felt herself blush.

"Our relationship is entirely professional," she said in a tone that belied her words. "What about you? It's not easy having a relationship when you're working all hours, is it?"

To her surprise, a beatific smile spread across Hall's face.

"Actually, I have a boyfriend, and I've recently found out that I'm pregnant!"

"That's amazing!" Amy exclaimed. "Congratulations! How far on are you?"

"Only fourteen weeks. At first, we kept it quiet because it can easily go wrong during the first stage, and I knew that the moment my mother heard the good news, she would start knitting baby clothes and buying things for the baby, so we held back until the first three months were over. We were also unsure how my boyfriend's mother would react. She had made it clear more than once that she thought that I was not good enough for her son."

Amy laughed incredulously. "*You*, not good enough? What is he – a member of the royal family?"

"Not quite, but, according to her, the next Conservative prime minister. His name is Charles Omerton. Maybe you have heard of him? He is the MSP for North Fife," Hall said, unable to hide her pride.

"Sorry, it's my colleague who is in charge of politics at the magazine, and I don't tend to follow MSPs on Twitter," Amy admitted.

Hall laughed. "I don't blame you. But Charles really is brilliant."

"So, what did his mother say about the baby?" Amy asked.

"It turned out to be the opposite of what we thought. She was over the moon. Now that she can see we are totally committed to each other, she is thrilled at the thought of becoming a granny. The other day, she took me to the SKYbar to celebrate the news."

Suddenly, Hall looked terribly sad.

"And you know, that was the last time I saw Martha. She happened to be there with Zane."

Amy put her hand over Hall's.

"Martha would want you to be happy and remember her as she was then. Let's keep in touch and find the bastard who killed her."

Chapter 9

That same morning found DI McCord and DC Calderwood on their way south to Galashiels.

Having finally left the congested roads of the city behind, they passed rolling hills shrouded in mist, lonely farmsteads and the occasional church steeple, its contours smudged by the heavy rain. A stream was running alongside the road for most of the way as if keeping them company.

Calderwood, immersed in his own thoughts, was looking out of the window, while McCord went over in his head what he wanted to find out about Godfrey Lomax and his construction company. Had Martha McGillivray visited him the day she died? McCord was sure of it. Calderwood had suggested phoning Lomax to check, but that would have lost them the element of surprise. What had McGillivray said to him? Had she threatened to expose some shady dealings? McCord did not expect Lomax to break down and confess in his first interview, but he wanted to see what kind of man they were dealing with. Was he involved in bribery and corruption – and murder? But the question that most persistently returned was what Amy Thornton was doing right now.

His thoughts were interrupted by Calderwood pointing out that they were nearing the village of Middleton.

"This must be close to where West Middleton is to be built, I suppose," said McCord. "There should be wonderful birdlife around here – probably partridges, plovers, perhaps even nightjars and owls at dusk." His wistfulness turned into anger. "And now they're going to ruin a beautiful place with yet another conglomeration of identikit housing estates."

Calderwood nodded. "I suppose you're right. But then, this area is ideal for commuters – cheaper homes and fast transport links into their workplace in the city."

They drove past a sign indicating Borthwick Castle, and McCord could not let the opportunity pass to tease Calderwood about his posh background.

"Isn't that your dad's pile?"

Calderwood feigned outrage. "Don't insult my family. That wouldn't even do as a weekend pad."

McCord laughed. "So, where did you grow up?"

"Morningside. Not exactly a castle."

"But not exactly slumming it either," McCord said.

He looked at the hills where he suspected Borthwick Castle to be.

"I'll bet the owners are not too happy about the West Middleton proposals. I wouldn't be, if I had a posh estate that was going to be next to a massive building site for years and then looking out on peasants' hovels spoiling my views."

"Shame the days have passed when landowners could simply send annoying people to a different continent," Calderwood said.

McCord sneaked a look across to Calderwood. "Your dad can't be too happy about you joining the police force."

Calderwood was quiet for a moment.

"He's not disinherited me, if that's what you mean. But he had other plans for me. A career in law, just like him, or at least business. Anything below chief constable will be a disappointment."

McCord nodded.

"It all depends on your starting point, I suppose. My dad thinks I'm a genius because I am a DI, and if I ever make it to chief inspector, he'll be beside himself with joy. Although I doubt that will happen while Gilchrist is in office. You, on the other hand, don't need to worry. You will definitely go far."

Calderwood bristled.

"See, you're doing it again. I don't want everybody to think, oh, yes, no wonder he got the promotion, after all, his dad is a judge. I want to get there on my own merit!"

McCord smiled.

"You will. And as long as you know that, to hell with other people."

The rain was coming down in sheets now and made it difficult for McCord to see more than a few yards ahead. The twisting and winding road required McCord to concentrate on his driving, so both men fell quiet again.

Eventually they reached the area to the west of the town centre, where both Lomax's headquarters and Galashiels Academy were signposted.

"Did you ever play against them?" Calderwood asked. "They used to be brilliant at rugby."

McCord pulled a face.

"I could never see the point chasing a ball that isn't even round and fighting over it with guys twice my size. I find birdwatching a lot more civilised."

McCord had never quite embraced the fact that he was only five feet ten and of a slim build, and he had often wondered if his fierce and sometimes aggressive pursuit of criminals was a reaction to this perceived deficit. He turned into a business park and found a parking spot close to the entrance of Lomax Construction.

"Well, let's see what Mr Lomax has to say for himself."

The front of the futuristic building consisted mainly of glass panels that gave a splendid view of an elegant spiral staircase and huge loops of electric lights inside. The other three sides of the building were covered with black panels and made it look like a container dotted with embrasures. Huddled into their jackets against the steady drizzle that had replaced the sheet rain, McCord and Calderwood approached the main entrance via the paved front yard that was decorated with lines of young trees of exactly the same height and planted at exactly the same distance apart.

"Pretty cool," Calderwood commented, pointing to the bright curved lights inside that contrasted favourably with the indistinct greyness outside.

McCord was unimpressed. "It'll be like a sauna in the summer. Big show for visitors, but the staff can't even look outside from their offices. I already dislike the guy, and I haven't even met him yet."

Calderwood grinned. "Clearly, your course on subconscious prejudices hasn't had much impact. But remember, it's not a criminal offence to have a taste in architecture that is different from yours."

"More's the pity," McCord grumbled, but a smile was playing around his eyes.

* * *

Godfrey Lomax greeted them cordially in his rather less stylish but comfortable office and offered them coffee. His pockmarked face could not by any stretch of the imagination be called handsome, but quick, darting eyes, a strong jawline and decisive movements told McCord that here was a man who was used to getting his own way.

"Please have a seat." Lomax's voice was a rich baritone; maybe this was nature's way of compensating him for his lack of good looks.

He pointed to a leather suite in the windowless corner of his office. "How can I help you?"

McCord sat down next to Calderwood, who had his notebook out. He crossed his legs, trying to appear relaxed, while closely watching Godfrey Lomax's face.

"We are investigating the death of Martha McGillivray," McCord said. "Did she come to see you the day before yesterday?"

"Martha McGillivray is dead?" Lomax was clearly taken aback at the news. Or, McCord wondered, was he merely a good actor?

"Did you not hear the announcement?" McCord asked, incredulously. "It was on the lunchtime news yesterday, and the papers are full of it this morning."

"I don't watch daytime TV, and I don't read the papers until the evening if at all. I'm a busy man," Lomax said.

There was a pause before he added, "That is very sad."

McCord, however, thought that he did not look terribly sad. He also noted the fact that Lomax had not asked the obvious question, namely how Martha McGillivray had died.

The secretary knocked and entered with a tray. There was an uncomfortable silence while she served the coffee, handed round the plate with the biscuits and, after a polite 'Thank you, Suzie' from her boss, withdrew again.

"Was Martha McGillivray here on Tuesday?" McCord repeated his original question.

"Yes, she was," Lomax replied, a little too quickly. "She disturbed my lunch hour, as a matter of fact. When was she killed?"

"We didn't say she was killed," McCord said, his detective's instincts alerted again.

Lomax lost his domineering countenance for a moment.

"I... I assumed since you, two CID detectives, are here... What happened to her then?"

McCord noted Lomax's discomfort with some satisfaction.

"We are not at liberty to say. Why did Martha McGillivray come here to see you?"

"She wanted to talk about the West Middleton project – again," Lomax said, irritation showing in his voice.

"Oh, yes," McCord said. "Building an entire commuter town – quite a catch for you that, isn't it?"

"It is," Lomax said proudly. "We'll be creating hundreds of new jobs and revitalising the whole area around Gorebridge."

"Still, I've heard that many people are not at all happy about the project," McCord said.

Lomax's smile was well-practised. "There are always people who object to change; it comes with the territory."

"What exactly did Martha McGillivray ask you?" McCord wanted to know.

The smile froze.

"She asked me, again, to comment on suggestions that there had been 'irregularities' in the awarding of the contract." Lomax took a sip of his coffee. "Basically, she was accusing me of corruption, and I told her to check with the Planning Committee before she printed anything to this effect because I would be suing her for defamation if she did."

"That must have been a nice cosy chat," said McCord. "Did she also ask you about the Environmental Impact Assessment?"

Lomax put his cup down with a clatter.

"Where are you getting all this from? I commissioned an independent, reputable firm to carry out that assessment. They found no reason why the project should not go ahead. I'm happy to share a copy of their report with you. When projects like ours are proposed, there are always some environmentalists who claim that some rare orchid grows there or that an even rarer bat is fluttering around the area to be developed. They're just hoping to stall the process, but there is nothing rare or precious to be concerned about. You can ask the company."

"We shall certainly be doing that," McCord said drily. "Despite the job opportunities, the locals are also not very happy, it seems. There have been meetings at the local village halls around the area of Gorebridge, angry letters to the MSP and newspapers and a petition as well."

"Signed by a mere two hundred people. These things often take on a momentum of their own. A few people start agitating, and then others jump on the bandwagon and fancy themselves as some sort of freedom fighters even if they have never been to the area we are going to build on. The most vocal opponents are middle-class, retired busybodies with too much time on their hands. They don't need the jobs that the project will bring."

Lomax stopped himself and watched Calderwood scribbling eagerly in his notebook.

"What was Martha McGillivray's angle then?" McCord asked.

"It's obvious, isn't it? She was a journalist; she was after a story. But there is no story, I can assure you, and I think she realised that in the end." Lomax sighed. "You see, she and her campaigner friends are suspicious of any change. They simply have no vision."

"And what is your vision, exactly?" McCord said.

Lomax seemed pleased to be asked.

"Have you ever been to the railhead at Tweedbank, where the line from Edinburgh comes to an abrupt end in the middle of nowhere?"

McCord shook his head, wondering where this was going.

"The old track to Carlisle is still intact. It really is only a matter of time before the line is completed all the way into England. With rocketing fuel prices now, it makes absolute sense to take people off the roads. You'll have experienced the A7 getting here, so you will know how slow that road can be. You can be stuck behind a lorry or a bus on that twisting road with no chance of getting past easily or quickly."

The irony of that remark was not lost on McCord, coming as it did from someone in the construction industry whose lorries probably caused more slow-moving traffic than any other vehicles. He exchanged a glance with Calderwood and opened his mouth to protest, but Godfrey Lomax on his favourite topic was like a runaway train.

"There will be huge construction jobs here when that work is authorised in a few years' time. Listen, I am truly sorry that this McGillivray woman is dead, but I really don't think I can be of any further assistance in your inquiries. And, after all, time is money!"

Lomax stood up, indicating the matter was settled and the meeting over.

McCord rose as well and shook Lomax's outstretched hand.

"Thank you, Mr Lomax," McCord said, trying not to wince under the steel-like grip, and put down his card on the coffee table. "If you do happen to think of anything else that might be pertinent to our inquiries, please get in touch."

On the way out, McCord and Calderwood stopped at the secretary's desk. After checking her boss's diary, Suzie confirmed that Mr Lomax had been in a meeting with a Ms McGillivray between one o'clock and one thirty on 15th November. Yes, she had brought Mr Lomax his coffee, but Ms McGillivray had asked for a glass of water. No, she had not heard any of the conversation. Of course, she would be in touch if she remembered anything else and was delighted to help.

* * *

"What do you think?" McCord asked Calderwood as they were walking back to the Juke.

"Not sure," Calderwood said. "He's certainly an astute businessman with far-reaching plans and great ambitions. He doesn't strike me as the type who gives up easily. If he would resort to murder, however, is another matter."

"And how would he have done it?" McCord thought aloud. "The murder took some degree of preparation and planning. McGillivray would not have made an appointment in advance, and she would not have warned him that she had damaging information concerning him and his business."

"Good point," Calderwood said. "But from what Lomax said, it wasn't the first time she had bothered him, and he probably expected it not to be the last."

McCord nodded. "I'm sure he was lying about the reason for McGillivray's visit. She wouldn't go to see him twice about the same accusation. What new information did McGillivray have two days ago that she didn't have before? Also, the loss of a three-hundred-million-pound project and potential exposure to criminal investigations are the most convincing motives we've had so far. At least we have confirmation that she was here the day she died."

"I wonder what else she has been up to while she was here. There is still half an hour unaccounted for between her visit to Lomax and the departure of the train," Calderwood said.

"You're right! She had some food and water on the train. Do we know where that came from?"

Calderwood quickly found the relevant page in his notebook. "The packaging on the crackers said, 'The Gala Baker'." He googled the name. "It's on the High Street."

Unlike Edinburgh, Galashiels offers ample and affordable parking, so McCord and Calderwood were soon speaking to the homely middle-aged woman in charge of Galashiels' premier bakery. After being shown a picture, she clearly remembered Martha McGillivray.

"You see," she explained. "She didn't really want to buy anything at all, she only wanted to use our customer toilet, but she looked so unwell, I could hardly refuse her, could I?"

"Did she say anything else to you?" Calderwood asked.

"She was in a desperate hurry to get to the loo, and I heard her retching, poor thing. When she came out, her face was deathly white," the woman replied. "Before she left, she bought a bottle of water and some crackers, but she didn't say anything. Is she in trouble?"

"Not anymore," McCord said cryptically. "Thank you. You've been very helpful."

* * *

As McCord was opening the car door, his phone rang.

"Dougal Johnstone here," a breathless voice said. "The guy with the laptop has called again. He wants the handover to happen today. I said I needed another day, but he is not going to wait until tomorrow. It's today or never, he said. I thought he sounded suspicious, so I agreed."

McCord sighed. "Pity. That gives us very little time."

"Yes, but I had already prepared the package, just in case," Johnstone said defensively.

"Good. What time and place did he suggest for the exchange?" McCord asked.

"At one o'clock, Princes Street Gardens, at the bin next to the statue of the Polish bear."

"At one?! That's in less than an hour!" McCord took a deep breath. "Okay, go there. I'll get some officers there asap. Don't worry, you won't see them, but they'll be there."

He hung up and called St Leonard's.

"Would Gayfield Square not be closer?" Calderwood asked.

McCord shook his head. "A little, but by the time I've explained it all to them, it'll be too late. Hello? DI McCord here. Get me PC Turner on the phone, quickly, please."

He was pacing up and down the pavement until PC Turner's excited voice sounded. "Yes, sir?"

"Take four other officers and cut off all escape routes round the Polish bear statue in Princes Street Gardens. Handover is at the bin next to the statue at one."

"At one?" PC Turner exclaimed.

"Yes," McCord said impatiently. "Probably to coincide with the one o'clock gun salute from the Castle esplanade. Everybody in plain clothes, obviously, and not to be seen until we have the laptop. Chop, chop."

"Yes, sir." PC Turner hung up.

"Good man that," McCord said to Calderwood. "Let's hope they get it together in time."

Chapter 10

While Amy was waiting for the state-of-the art coffeemaker in the office of *Forth Write* magazine to foam the milk for her second latte that morning, she observed with great affection Martin Eden, political editor and close friend, as he was putting the finishing touches to one of his cartoons. The magazine had been famous for them long before Amy appeared on the scene and livened things up with her penchant for crime investigations. It had even been suggested that many subscribers bought the magazine specifically for his acerbic but funny take on the political situation. Eventually, Martin lowered his pencil and looked up with that mixture of exhaustion and triumph which always followed a successful piece of satire.

"Coffee?" Amy called over to him as she emptied the used coffee grains into the compost bin. It had taken her months, but eventually she had found the patience to go through the interminable process of producing a coffee from this infernal machine.

"You are an angel, my darling," Martin twittered and headed for the coffee station.

Martin had made it his life's mission to 'combat the powers of beige', as he called it, and was never seen in any outfit with fewer than five bright colours unless he had discovered one so intense, such as today's shimmering purple, that it could fight the battle and win the war all by itself. His precisely drawn, thin, black eyebrows and puckered red lips gave him both a ridiculous and dangerous air, which he cunningly used to his advantage during political interviews. By the time the hapless politicians had decided what they thought of this strange bird that was asking unpleasant questions, they had told him much more than they had intended.

Amy placed a cup under the spout, filled the little metal sieve with ground coffee and slid it into place before pouring the foamed milk onto her espresso.

"What do you know about a politician called Charles Omerton?" Amy asked.

Martin spread his arms wide.

"What *don't* I know about Charles Omerton, you should ask. As it happens, I am working on an article about him." He looked at Amy with mock suspicion. "*Very* dishy. Could be tempted myself if he weren't a Conservative. Don't tell me you are cheating in mind on our good friend DI McCord?"

"Good friend McCord!" she snorted. "He threw me out of St Leonard's, remember? I've never felt so humiliated in my whole life!"

"If I recall the content of yesterday's tantrum correctly, it was the superintendent who had forbidden McCord to cooperate with you on this case. What is the poor man to do? I'm sure he is pining for you as we speak."

"Ach, stop it," Amy said. "Since when does he do what he is told by Gilchrist?"

"Well, last time he didn't, he was sent on leave and made to attend some ghastly re-education courses, wasn't he?" Martin reminded her. "He needs to tread carefully, does DI McCord."

"Why are you so damned reasonable? You're my friend, you're supposed to be on my side!"

"Always, my darling," he said, "I'm at your side with the sword of truth and words of wisdom."

Amy sighed. "And Charles Omerton?"

"Charles is the glowing ember that is going to herald the rebirth of the Scottish Conservative Party like the proverbial Phoenix from the ashes," Martin said. "Modest background, scholarship to St Nicodemus', a small private school in the West End, First Class Honours in Politics, Philosophy and Economics from Edinburgh University. For a blue badge, he presents himself as fairly progressive on social and green issues. Clever, well-mannered and destined for great things, if you ask me."

"Shame he got his girlfriend pregnant," Amy added with some relish.

Martin's dark pinhead eyes widened.

"How do you know *that*?"

"I happened to be chatting with her this morning," Amy said casually.

Martin applauded her ironically. "Anyway, nowadays little human transgressions like that seem to endear a candidate to younger Conservative voters who don't want their leaders to be too virtuous. Has he proposed to her yet?"

"Don't think so."

Martin tutted. "Very modern, and possibly politically risqué, too."

"Maybe you should give your article a more personal twist, by including some juicy information on his private life," Amy said. "That would make him a lot more interesting to some of our readers, anyway."

Martin pulled a face. "I don't like dirty linen politics, you know that."

"There's no need for that," Amy said, "but a well-rounded picture of the man? Definitely a winner. At least as long as there is something more to him than a career-obsessed robot."

"Well, if you find me something exciting, I'll share the by-line with you."

"Deal."

She would have to dig deeper into Kirsty's life anyway, so she might as well kill two birds with one stone.

* * *

McCord and Calderwood had passed Eskbank when PC Turner confirmed that he and three officers in plain clothes were in position around the war memorial in Princes Street Gardens, which consists of a life-size bronze statue of Wojtek the bear and a frieze depicting him with Polish soldiers during WWII. It was twelve forty-five, and dark clouds threatened more rain. McCord was drumming impatiently on the steering wheel and kept looking at the screen of his phone that was fixed between him and Calderwood in front of the dashboard.

"We'll hear nothing until after one," Calderwood said. "We might as well relax."

McCord did not dignify this with a response. Instead, he put his foot down to overtake a construction lorry he had been stuck behind for the last ten miles.

The drive to Edinburgh seemed to take forever. At one fifteen they were still negotiating the traffic on the outskirts of the city.

"What the hell is going on in the Gardens?" McCord muttered. "The exchange should have happened by now."

Just then McCord's phone rang. Both he and Calderwood reached for the green icon, but McCord was faster, although he almost bumped into the Skoda in front of him.

"PC Turner? You got it?"

"Negative," PC Turner muttered, and they could hear the frustration in his voice.

McCord struggled to stay calm.

"What happened?"

"You won't believe it, sir," PC Turner began. "A couple of PCs from Gayfield Square turned up a few minutes before one, wandering along the path. The target never showed up. He must have been spooked. Sorry, sir."

"Not your fault, PC Turner," McCord said, trying not to show his disappointment. "Get everybody back to the station; I don't think he'll risk it now."

He called off.

"Damn. You were right, Calderwood, I should have called Gayfield Square and warned them. It never occurred to me that they'd be wandering around there at that time. Aren't people always moaning that there aren't enough bobbies on the beat?"

* * *

Back at St Leonard's, McCord had an uncomfortable meeting with Superintendent Gilchrist. At the end of his report, McCord praised PC Turner for getting the officers in place so quickly.

"It is certainly not *his* fault," Gilchrist said pointedly. "Let's hope that the CCTV gives us something useful."

McCord nodded, quite relieved. He had expected worse and was pleasantly surprised at the Super's unusually sensible response.

"On it, sir," McCord said and hastily withdrew.

Chapter 11

Having missed lunch at the canteen, McCord was polishing off a sandwich at his desk, when DC Sutton's text alert pinged on his screen. He jumped up and rushed to her workstation. Outside, he forced himself to knock and wait for her permission to enter.

Instead of continuing to type as she normally would, she turned her long, horse-like face towards McCord and looked at him with her green eyes that were huge behind her lenses.

"What have you got, DC Sutton?" he said encouragingly.

She handed him the West Middleton papers she had been working through.

"Councillor Weatherspoon. One of the signatories in the planning permission for Lomax's project. Heavily in debt. Wife likes shopping, son and daughter at private school."

"Any monies coming in from Lomax?" McCord asked hopefully.

"Not yet. Maybe into a different account," DC Sutton replied in her inimitable, concise style.

"Great job. Keep looking."

McCord was almost back out in the open-plan office when something occurred to him. He weaved his way back into her den.

"We don't have a warrant for this," he reminded her. "As I said, nothing illegal, at least not yet."

DC Sutton shrugged without moving her eyes from the screen.

"Can't be traced," she said.

Her fingers flew across the keys with incredible speed, and McCord was fairly sure that DC Sutton had already forgotten he was there.

* * *

Encouraged by DC Sutton's find, McCord asked PC Dharwan to brief him on Martha McGillivray's investigation into the West Middleton project. McGillivray had certainly been thorough, but despite the many accusations and suspicions mentioned in the files, PC Dharwan had found no evidence of any illegal activity. Yet, if Martha McGillivray had not found anything, why on earth had she gone to the trouble and expense to speak with Lomax for a second time? McCord had the distinct feeling that they were missing some vital clue.

His thoughts were interrupted by an imperious clanging on the door. Superintendent Gilchrist's tall, immaculately dressed figure almost filled the door frame.

"My office, DI McCord. Now, please."

Leaving a worried-looking Calderwood behind, McCord followed his superior down the corridor, wondering what the Super's problem was this time.

As the door of Gilchrist's office clanked shut behind McCord, he braced himself for what was to come.

"Do you know what the consequences are of deliberately ignoring my orders?" Gilchrist thundered. "Did I or did I not tell you explicitly that there were to be no more cosy chats with Miss Thornton?"

He paused and looked at McCord, waiting for an answer.

"You did, sir," McCord said.

"Why then do I see her name on the visitors' log next to yesterday's date? Why?"

His face was the colour of puce.

"She got past the duty sergeant and suddenly appeared in my office," McCord explained calmly. "As it turned out, she had information pertinent to our inquiry, which she had a duty to share with the police. As soon as she had delivered it, I told her that our cooperation had to stop and asked her to leave. If you check the signing out sheet, sir, you will notice that she was here for five minutes at the most, and we have had no contact with her since."

Mollified, Gilchrist leaned back in his chair.

"And I expect that to continue. Let's hope that none of the other hacks spotted her coming or going. Well, don't waste any more time chatting. We have a killer to catch, so get on with it!"

McCord turned round without another word and left. In moments like these, he empathised deeply with a killer.

* * *

When McCord returned to the office, livid at Gilchrist's petty treatment of him, Calderwood eyed him curiously, but McCord just shrugged and shook his head in a silent reply. No need to go into the detail of Gilchrist's senseless outburst. Calderwood did not press him for details, for he had some exciting news. He waved an evidence bag and a wad of papers at McCord.

"McGillivray's phone," he declared triumphantly. "No detectable fingerprints apart from hers, but it is unlocked, and we've got a printout of her deleted messages and emails from the last four weeks before her death."

McCord grabbed the phone.

"At last. I'll take this, and you have a look at the deleted stuff."

McCord touched the email icon. He scrolled quickly through the first dozen from online shops, a cruise company, reminders from HMRC urging her to fill in her self-assessment tax form and invitations to make an appointment with her dentist. There were also emails from the Stop West Middleton campaign updating their recipients on the progress, or rather lack thereof, in the fight against the project. Eventually, the name Blackford & Sons caught his eye.

"Wasn't Blackford & Sons the name of the solicitors McGillivray used for her will?" McCord asked.

Calderwood looked up from the ream of papers and nodded. "What is the email about?"

"Blablabla, this is to confirm the time of our meeting on 20th November at 10.30am etc.," McCord read. "I wonder what that meeting was about. Give them a call and put them on speaker phone."

While McCord was working his way backwards through McGillivray's inbox, Calderwood's call was forwarded to Mr John Blackford, the senior partner of Blackford & Sons, who told him very politely and with a hint of surprise that they could not give confidential information about their clients over the phone even if they claimed to be police.

"Of course," Calderwood said, embarrassed. "Please, phone St Leonard's police station and ask for DI McCord, the inspector in charge of the investigation into Martha McGillivray's murder. DI McCord would like to know what the arranged meeting on the 20th was about. If you prefer, you can always come to the station in person," he added evenly while winking at McCord.

"There is no need for that," Mr Blackford said pleasantly. "I'll get the file and call back immediately."

He hung up.

McCord smiled. "Well played. He wouldn't like to lose the three hundred pounds per hour he can charge a client by coming here."

A few minutes later, McCord's landline rang, and the solicitor's call was put through.

"John Blackford, from Blackford & Sons. Your colleague told me that Ms McGillivray has been murdered? Is this true?"

McCord confirmed this.

"Shocking!" the lawyer exclaimed. "I want, of course, to assist in any way I can. How can I help?"

"We have found her will, stating that her assets should go to Zane Smith, her boyfriend, and a former colleague, Kirsty Hall. But now it has come to our attention that she had arranged a meeting with you for the 20th," McCord said.

"Yes, she had requested a meeting as she had asked me to draft a new will, and she was supposed to sign it on the 20th," Blackford confirmed.

"And who benefits from that new will?" McCord asked, looking at Calderwood who was trying to follow the conversation.

"Well, I was surprised when she told me," the solicitor said. "According to the new will, all of her assets were to go to the periodical *Private Eye* with the stipulation that they investigate corruption in Scotland."

McCord whistled through his teeth. "Did she say why?"

"She only said that she was disappointed in both previous beneficiaries and wanted to be sure that investigative journalism was kept alive," said Blackford.

"But who inherits now that she has not been able to sign the new will?" McCord asked.

"The expressed wishes of the deceased are usually taken into consideration, but when it comes down to it, a signed will trumps any changes of mind, even in writing."

"Thank you very much, Mr Blackford. Could you email me a copy of the new will? Send it to mccord@policescotland.org.uk, yes, mc without an 'a', all lower case. I'm afraid the beneficiaries will have to wait until the investigation is concluded. We couldn't allow a murderer to profit from their crime, could we, Mr Blackford? Thank you. Goodbye."

McCord looked triumphantly at Calderwood.

"A few more days, and Zane Smith would have lost a tidy little nest egg. I think McGillivray's sour face on the cruise had nothing to do with the dress she was wearing; their relationship was breaking down because after a week cooped up in a small cabin with Zane she must have realised what a wet rag he is."

"You conveniently forget that Kirsty Hall also benefitted from the old will. She stood to lose as much as he did," Calderwood pointed out.

"But, unlike our ageing model, Miss Hall has a proper job, and she is carrying a baby. Surely, you don't seriously think–"

"Just because a woman is pregnant, it doesn't mean that she turns into a saint," Calderwood said. "Besides, having a baby won't do her career any good."

"Well, I suppose you should check out both of them," McCord conceded. "Has Smith come in to give us his statement yet?"

Calderwood did not reply. Something in the printouts had caught his eye.

"Calderwood?"

"Sorry," Calderwood said. "Look at these deleted texts. Dozens of messages to McGillivray from a guy called Cameron Coates. Really nasty stuff. 'You need a real man to teach you some respect, you bitch', 'someone should shove your articles down your throat until you choke on them' and so it goes on."

"Charming guy! We certainly need to check him out," McCord said. "Could be empty words of course, but–"

He broke off when PC Dharwan knocked on his open door.

"I thought you should see this, sir," she said and handed him the evening edition of the *Edinburgh Messenger*.

'COUNCIL CORRUPTION LINKED TO MURDER OF JOURNALIST' screamed the headline. The article mentioned all the misgivings regarding the West Middleton project that Martha McGillivray had detailed in her files but also revealed that Godfrey Lomax was married to the elder daughter of Councillor Weatherspoon, who had been instrumental in awarding the contract. Surely, at best a conflict of interest and crass nepotism; at worst, corruption worthy of a banana republic, the article suggested. And now, the very same journalist who had been on their case was conveniently dead. Hopefully, the police would now take a greater interest in the business practices of Lomax Construction as well as the inner workings of the council. And then the by-line: Kirsty Hall.

McCord threw the paper on Calderwood's desk, so that he could read it for himself.

"Where the hell did she get that information from?" McCord asked in his dangerously quiet voice. "Did *she* lift McGillivray's laptop? But then, why would she try to sell it to her own newspaper? It doesn't make any sense. PC Dharwan, tell PC Turner to check the CCTV specifically for Kirsty Hall, and Zane Smith as well, while he's at it."

PC Dharwan nodded and hurried off.

Calderwood looked smug.

"Shall I *haul* her in then?" he asked with a grin.

"Yes," McCord said, "and cut out the puns."

McCord was still digesting the news that a vulnerable, pregnant woman had pulled the wool over his eyes when the phone rang. It was the duty sergeant.

"Zane Smith is at reception."

"Excellent," McCord said, brightening up. "Put him in Interview Room 1. I'll be down in a minute."

* * *

Zane Smith looked very uncomfortable on the plastic chair pulled up to the chipped Formica table. The harsh light accentuated the deep lines that had begun to form around his eyes and mouth.

McCord watched him through the spyhole for just long enough to make him worry, but not long enough to give him any reason to complain.

Calderwood switched on the recorder and went through the usual introduction routine.

"Now, Mr Smith," McCord said brightly. "Thank you for coming in."

"I just wanted to drop off my statement as you asked." Smith's voice had a whiny undertone. "I didn't know I was going to be interrogated."

"We have only a few questions for you about certain developments that have come to light," McCord said.

He waited a few seconds to let the anxiety kick in.

"What developments?" Smith asked. "I haven't done anything wrong!"

"Nobody said you had," McCord replied calmly. "We simply wanted your perspective on a few details of the case. First of all, when did you find out that Martha was intending to cut you out of her will?"

McCord noted with satisfaction that damp patches began to appear under Smith's arms.

"I don't know anything about that," Smith pleaded. "I wasn't even sure that I was in her will in the first place."

"But when we spoke to you before, you said that Martha told you that you would be provided for when she died."

"I know, but she never gave me any specific details, and Martha could be quite… mischievous sometimes. I was wondering if she was just teasing me to see my reaction."

McCord's facial expression made it quite clear that he did not believe a word.

"Hm. Not exactly a sign of a close, loving relationship, would you say? And lo and behold, a few days before she is due to sign the new will, leaving you with nothing, she is dead."

Zane Smith's eyes darted from McCord to Calderwood, and seeing no sympathy in either face, he leaned back in his chair.

"I'm not saying another word without a lawyer," he declared. "I made my statement detailing my whereabouts in the two days before the murder. I have never done anything to harm Martha, so you won't be able to prove that I have. Can I go now?"

"You can, Mr Smith," McCord said, "but, please, don't leave town without notifying us."

Smith stood up hesitantly as if he could not quite believe that he was being allowed to leave. Walking unnaturally straight, he made his way to the door.

When he had disappeared down the corridor, McCord smiled cheerlessly.

"Challenge accepted."

Chapter 12

Amy had unobtrusively followed Cameron Coates from the *Edinburgh Messenger* offices to The Shamrock, an Irish pub on the Cowgate. In medieval times, herds of cattle had jostled their way along this street to the city market; now it was the tourists who were getting slaughtered. Entering the pub a few seconds behind Coates, Amy was faced with green banners plastering the walls and Irish folk songs blasting from a crackling sound system.

She felt a twinge of nostalgia. It was here only eight months ago that a spate of murders had begun leading her and McCord on a hunt for a serial killer. Together, they had solved the case, and the publication of a special edition in the *Forth Write* magazine had made her the talk of the town for a while. And now, here she was all on her own, no longer welcome at St Leonard's, and finding herself missing the constant squabbling with McCord and the smell of cheap instant coffee and waxed linoleum at the police station.

Coates seemed to be a regular in the pub as the barman greeted him by name, and Amy hoped that he had not arranged to meet anybody else. He nodded to a few of the other punters but none of them seemed in a hurry to join him at his table. Amy ordered a gin and tonic at the bar and sat there for a while sipping the pink fizz with what she hoped was a suggestive sensuality until she was sure that he had noticed her.

The way he eyed her up was not exactly subtle and confirmed her first impression of an unremarkable, middle-aged man vain enough to believe that an attractive young woman would be trying to catch his eye.

After a decent interval, she descended with a sinuous movement of her legs and hips from her bar stool, making sure that he could see the perfectly tailored dress hugging her slim figure, and moved hesitantly towards his table.

"Are you Cameron Coates?" she asked with disarming shyness.

"That's me." He licked the foam off his strangely shapeless lips. "And who are you, pretty lady?"

Normally, she would have been miffed at not being recognised but in this case, she was relieved.

"I'm Amy," she said breathlessly, "and I'm *such* a fan. Your article on the rise in bin collection fees was brilliant. Holding those council bureaucrats to account, sharp but witty at the same time!"

The article had been turgid, but Amy always did her homework.

Cameron Coates gave a self-satisfied smile.

"Thank you, it was a very minor thing on the side."

"Really? What are you working on now?" Amy asked, feigning interest.

"If I told you, I'd have to kill you," he said, touching his fleshy nose.

Amy struggled to keep a straight face.

"Then I won't ask. I suppose you must be devastated about your colleague Martha McGillivray's death. It was in the papers that she worked for the *Edinburgh Messenger* as well."

Coates turned his pint on the mat.

"Well," he said, his smile fading, "she was not really employed at the paper, you know, she was just freelance."

"Ah, really?" Amy looked at him wide-eyed as if hoping for more insider knowledge. "The article I read made out that she was an amazing journalist."

"They always say that when somebody dies, don't they," he spat. "Have you ever read an obituary saying the deceased was a nasty little bitch?"

Amy covered her mouth in mock horror.

"But she wasn't like that, was she?"

"Let's say she was very good at elbowing other people out of her way. She used to be married to this journalist, Shug McCain, a great guy, but when they were abroad together on assignments, she always took the credit for all the stories that came back. Always me, me, me, that was Martha McGillivray. And when she had no use for Shug anymore, she divorced him and screwed him right over. But don't tell people I said that because for some reason, half the world seems to think she was a bloody saint."

His knuckles were white when he grabbed the glass and took a big swig.

Amy proclaimed to be shocked.

"She didn't steal any of your stories, though, did she?"

Coates sighed and, like a martyr to heaven, looked up at the swathes of green fabric covering the ceiling.

"Ach, what's the use of regretting the past. Especially, if the present is so delightful!"

He toasted Amy, who sucked on her environmentally friendly straw which had already begun to disintegrate.

"Do you know how she died?" she asked conspiratorially. "The official statement from the police was very vague."

"Well, they have to be careful what they say," he explained as if she was a child or an idiot. "But I heard from my informants that she died in the toilet of that train she was found in and that it was a very painful death. Agony apparently."

"Really?" Amy said, open-mouthed. "It must be amazing to know so much more than ordinary people about what's happening in the world."

He smiled.

"It can also be a great burden," he declared. "Are you thinking of becoming a journalist yourself?"

"Well, I've written a couple of articles for a fashion magazine," Amy lied blithely, "but my dream is to be a proper investigative journalist like you. Would you mind terribly showing me some of your stuff and how you go about finding out things?"

Coates' smile was getting broader by the minute, showing yellow teeth.

"I have a very nice bottle of wine at home waiting to be drunk by a beautiful young lady. And at the same time, we can make a start to launching your new career. What do you say?"

What a creep, Amy thought, but her answer betrayed nothing but enthusiasm.

"I'd love to. Thank you so much!"

As she was following Coates out of the pub, she slipped her right hand into her coat pocket where her fingers felt the reassuring cylindrical shape of her mace spray.

* * *

"Calderwood, check this out!"

McCord held out Martha McGillivray's phone.

"This is the very last message she wrote. She probably collapsed before she could click on the send button. It was meant for Kirsty Hall."

"'Lo arch dig gill'," Calderwood read aloud. "What the hell does that mean? Lo surely is Lomax. Which arch are we supposed to dig under? And who is this Gill?"

"Not a clue," McCord said. "Why do I have the impression that Kirsty Hall knows a lot more than she is telling us?"

McCord took a picture of the screen and scrolled further back.

"They met up quite frequently. Here, four weeks ago, Kirsty writes: 'I've got exciting news, can't wait to tell you!' I wonder if that was about the pregnancy."

He checked earlier messages but saw nothing that gave a clue to McGillivray's murder.

"What about the messages from Zane Smith?" Calderwood asked.

McCord grunted. "Okay. Let's see what our model texted McGillivray about."

He opened the text messages and read them backwards in time.

"Hm," he grunted as he read. "Thought so."

"What is it?" Calderwood demanded impatiently.

"Questions, questions, questions and whingeing. 'Where are you? Why did you not come to see me? I made dinner especially. Why can't you come tonight? You promised etc. etc. etc.' Her standard reply: work, work, work. A guy like that simply doesn't understand the demands of a job like hers."

"Maybe McGillivray was playing away? And work was just an excuse?"

"There are no messages here to suggest that," McCord said. "And, anyway, she wouldn't do that."

"You assume a lot about a woman you have never met, don't you?"

McCord waved Calderwood's misgivings away. "I have the strangest feeling... it is as if I knew her, and as if she is trying to tell me something."

"She tried to tell Kirsty Hall who killed her," Calderwood said. "I think it's time to concentrate on Godfrey Lomax and leave poor Zane to his grief."

McCord scowled. "And his half of a Portobello flat."

"Are there any messages from people connected to the West Middleton project?" Calderwood asked, deflecting McCord from his obsession with Smith.

McCord tapped on the screen.

"There is a WhatsApp group called Stop West Middleton." He read through the thread for a while. "Meetings, news about letters to and from the council, campaign stuff; nothing to suggest violence or illegality. Must have been a pain in the butt for Lomax, though. They really tried everything, and one of them seems to be a lawyer. McGillivray was spurring them on every time; here, she promises them maximum publicity if they come up with something tangible against Lomax. Reading between the lines, it looks as if she still hadn't found proof of criminal wrongdoing when she wrote that."

There was a knock on the door.

"Kirsty Hall is here to see you," PC Dharwan told McCord.

McCord jumped up.

"At last. Put her in an interview room, whichever one is free. Won't be long," he told her. "Come on, Calderwood, it's time to play good cop, bad cop, and this time, I'll be the bad cop."

* * *

Kirsty Hall was in a defiant mood.

"You can hardly accuse me of withholding evidence from the police when I publish everything I know in my newspaper," she said after McCord had given her a hard time about her article.

"I don't think you fully understand the situation you are in," Calderwood explained calmly. "You publish information that purportedly comes from Martha McGillivray, but which is nowhere to be found in her possessions. Her laptop was stolen around the time she died, and so far, we have been unable to find the person who took it from the train. We are now wondering if you were there when Martha died, and if perhaps you have her laptop. You had a strong motive for wanting Martha out of the way."

"Actually, two motives," McCord interjected, pulling his chair forward and making a show of scrutinizing her face.

Kirsty looked stunned.

"What motive would I have to kill Martha? She was my friend!"

"A much closer friend than you made us believe," McCord said. "You are one of the main beneficiaries of her will – a tidy sum, I might add, which you would have lost if Martha had lived a few days longer."

McCord wondered if the surprise on her face was genuine.

"I didn't know I was in her will," Hall insisted. "And what do you mean, I would have lost it if she had lived longer?"

"Martha had made an appointment with her solicitor to change the will. Both you and Zane Smith were to be cut out. She wanted everything to go to *Private Eye*."

McCord eyed her closely, but Hall betrayed no feeling but confusion.

"I suppose it was not surprising that Martha put Zane and me in her will. There was nobody else she was close to. But why would she cut us both out of it?"

"Are you really telling me that you didn't know anything about either will?" McCord asked.

"That's exactly what I'm saying," Hall shot back. "And now could you explain what the second motive is that I'm supposed to have?"

McCord stood up so he could tower over her.

"Well, you've just proved that yourself. Now that Martha is dead, you are free to expose the West Middleton scandal and make your name as a serious journalist, well, a journalist, anyway. And now I'm asking you, and remember this interview is recorded and might be used in evidence: did you take Martha McGillivray's laptop from the train while Martha was dying or already dead in the toilet?"

"I did not!" Hall screeched. She was close to tears. "I had nothing to do with her death!"

"Then where did you get that information in the newspaper about Councillor Weatherspoon?"

Hall pressed her lips together. McCord motioned to Calderwood to intervene.

"If you are innocent, Miss Hall, you must help us to understand, so *we* can help *you*," Calderwood said kindly.

McCord watched a battle going on in Kirsty's mind.

"Telling the truth does not come easy to you, does it?" McCord teased her. "I suppose that's a professional hazard."

Hall threw a hostile look at McCord.

"I got the information from Martha's flat."

McCord had not expected that response.

"How did you manage to do that?" Calderwood asked. "We searched the flat and took all her paperwork away. Shortly afterwards, the flat was sealed off because the forensics team were searching for–" he caught himself in time "–for evidence."

Hall shrugged.

"I went to Martha's flat straight after your visit to the *Messenger*," she said. "I've still got a key, and I knew that she kept a backup of all her files on a USB stick hidden inside the *Guide to Greece*. She told me a year ago to get it if something should happen to her and to publish whatever was on it."

"And where is this USB stick now?" McCord demanded to know.

Hall hesitated.

"It is an important piece of evidence in a murder inquiry. You can either hand it over now, or an officer will accompany you to your flat to retrieve it," McCord told her.

Hesitantly, Hall opened her bag, pulled out the stick from a zipped-up compartment and put it on the table.

"Was she worried about someone trying to kill her?" McCord asked.

Hall shook her head.

"Not anyone in particular, I don't think, but she said to me once that it was a dangerous business we worked in, and always to be careful."

Her eyes shone with tears.

McCord and Calderwood exchanged a look. McCord was doubtful but nodded.

Calderwood took a print from the case file and placed it in front of Hall.

"There was a message on Martha's phone that she composed seconds before she died. She meant to send it to you, but she was not able to complete it."

Hall stared at the message. "Lo – Lomax? She was trying to warn me about Lomax?"

"We were hoping you could tell us," Calderwood said. "What arch did she mean, and who is this woman Gill?"

"I have no idea," Hall said, "it doesn't make any sense."

"Well, think about it," McCord told her sternly. "And let us know if anything occurs to you. But if even a hint of a suggestion of this text message or any part of our conversation appears in one of your articles, you will be charged with obstruction."

"It might be wise to watch your back as Martha advised until we have gotten to the bottom of this," Calderwood added, in a more conciliatory tone.

"Yes," said McCord, "at the very least, Lomax will sue you for defamation because of your article unless we can prove he's a killer."

Hall sighed.

"I'm sure that Lomax and Weatherspoon have something to hide," she said, "but I never thought they would resort to murder. I'm sorry now that I sent your friend on a wild goose chase."

McCord frowned.

"What friend?"

Hall winked. "We all know that Amy Thornton is more than that but–"

"What has Miss Thornton got to do with any of this?" McCord's voice suddenly had a new edge to it.

"Oh, I thought you knew," Kirsty said. "Amy is investigating Cameron Coates, a colleague of mine at the *Messenger*; in fact, she is meeting him tonight, well, I say 'meeting', more like waylaying him–"

"Where?"

McCord expelled air from his nose like a bull in front of a red rag.

Hall was clearly worried now.

"He usually goes to The Shamrock, an Irish–"

"I know The Shamrock," McCord interrupted her. "When?"

"He goes there most days after work, so they're probably there right now," she said anxiously.

McCord stopped the recording and rose from his chair.

"Remember what I said. Every bit of new information you happen to find comes to us, not the *Messenger*, and let us know if you have to leave town. No doubt, we will speak soon. Goodbye, Miss Hall."

He motioned to a PC who was standing in the corridor to show Hall to the exit and turned to Calderwood.

"The Shamrock. Now."

Chapter 13

The journey through the city centre was tortuous.

"We'd have been faster walking," McCord growled, fruitlessly revving the engine every time a few inches of free space appeared in front of them.

"What did you make of Kirsty Hall? Do you still think she is a suspect?" Calderwood asked.

McCord realised Calderwood was trying to take their minds off Amy's meeting with Coates.

"Absolutely," McCord played along, grateful for the distraction. "She benefits from McGillivray's death, she is ambitious, manipulative and not above breaking the law if she thinks she can get away with it."

"But what about McGillivray's text? It more or less tells us who the killer is, and surely her sending it to Hall shows that McGillivray trusted Hall," Calderwood said.

"Strictly speaking, the text only tells us who she *thought* killed her," McCord replied. "Maybe she regarded Hall as some sort of surrogate daughter and did not see that she had her own agenda."

"But McGillivray must have been disillusioned with Hall," Calderwood said. "The solicitor told you that McGillivray was disappointed in both Smith and Hall, and that is why she wanted to cut them out of her will."

"I wonder what she was disappointed about," McCord said. "Hall has certainly not been straight with us. She must have known that something in their relationship had changed, and she did not tell us."

"True," Calderwood said. "She also had opportunity. If they were both so close, she could easily have poisoned McGillivray, especially when McGillivray did not suspect her at all. And Smith said they all had champagne at the SKYbar."

"Which is where Smith could have poisoned her as well," McCord pointed out. "Did Hall not say she was there with her future mother-in-law? Maybe the mother-in-law saw something at the SKYbar without realising its significance. We'll have to interview her, and the staff at the bar as well."

* * *

Eventually, they reached the Cowgate. McCord slapped his parking permit on the dashboard and simply abandoned his Juke on the pavement outside The Shamrock.

The pub was busy with people enjoying an after-work refreshment, but the owner recognised McCord immediately from a previous investigation. Although the pub had been compelled to close for a day to allow for forensics to gather evidence, the ensuing murder tourism had more than made up for the initial loss of revenue. The owner approached the detectives who were scanning the room, trying to see past punters who were standing around and blocking the view of the tables along the walls.

"DI McCord, isn't it? How can I help you today? A pint of Guinness?"

"We're here on business, I'm afraid. We are hoping to speak to a regular customer of yours, Cameron Coates. We're not sure what he looks like, but he was probably here with a short, slim, dark-haired woman. Pretty," he added with a side glance at Calderwood.

"Unfortunately, you've just missed them," the landlord said. "Quite a striking young lady. They had a drink over there at the window. I had the impression that they had met for the first time here, and then they left together, quite chummy." He came closer and lowered his voice. "Which surprised me a bit, if you know what I mean."

"Do you know where they went?" McCord asked, already turning to go.

"No idea, sorry. You sure you don't want to stay for a pint? It's on the house!"

But the detectives were rushing out of the door, McCord holding his phone to his ear. He let it ring until it went to voice messages.

"Amy, McCord here. Be careful around Coates. Get away from him as soon as you can."

He paused as if he wanted to say more but just pressed the red icon.

"How can she be so stupid?" McCord fumed, yanking open the door of the Juke. "Meeting a murder suspect on her own and then going off with him! Where does this guy live?"

"I don't know," Calderwood said, panic creeping into his voice.

"For God's sake!" McCord shouted, dialling a familiar number. "DC Sutton? McCord here. We need an address for a Cameron Coates, Edinburgh. Asap. Thanks."

He hung up, pacing up and down the pavement, only stopping once to send Amy a message. Maybe it was more likely she would see that than listen to her voicemails. After what seemed an eternity, his phone pinged. He read the message on the screen.

"Let's go!"

* * *

Number twenty-one Blackmoor Street stood in a row of run-down blocks of flats with weed-infested front gardens where the only splashes of colour came from discarded Irn-Bru bottles and empty crisp packets, blown in by the wind and trapped inside the wire mesh fences.

"This is only a stopgap," Cameron Coates said. "I'm saving up for a place in Leith Walk."

Amy guessed that flattery always impressed people like Coates.

"House prices in Edinburgh are astronomical. You're doing well having your own place. I still live in my mum's flat."

He pushed open the battered front door and led the way up a concrete stairwell adorned with graffiti and stained take-away cartons. Amy watched the shapeless form of his bomber jacket above a similarly shapeless bottom moving ahead of her. A little voice in her head whispered 'run', but, as always, curiosity got the better of her.

"Bloody junkies," Coates muttered, breathing heavily from the exertion of climbing up the stairs. "I've been on to the landlord for months about fixing that entrance. But there is no need to be afraid," he reassured Amy. "Even if there are some junkies here, they wouldn't dare hurt you when I'm around."

"That's a huge relief," Amy said, trying to keep the sarcasm out of her voice.

The flat was surprisingly well furnished and clean if not particularly tidy. Coates hastily cleared some mail and magazines from the leather sofa and invited Amy to sit.

"Sorry, if I had expected such a pretty visitor, I would have made more of an effort to tidy up. How about that glass of wine now?"

"Lovely," Amy said. "Actually, I'm quite hungry. Any chance of a snack?"

"I'll see what I can rustle up." Coates moved towards the tiny kitchen.

"Can I use your bathroom?" Amy called after him.

"Of course, make yourself at home," he shouted.

Amy rushed out into the hall. The bathroom was to her left. The next room was clearly the only bedroom. Through the half-open door, she could see an unmade double bed, a bedside table and the edge of a wardrobe which took up almost all the remaining floor space. Beyond the bedroom was a closed door. Coates was rummaging in the kitchen, so Amy tiptoed up to the door and turned the old-fashioned knob. She jumped at the creaking sound it made and listened. It was quiet in the kitchen, but then she heard the clinking of glass. Resolutely, she opened the door to what had been intended as a broom cupboard. But what the dim hall light revealed, made her freeze. The walls were plastered with newspaper cuttings and photos of Martha McGillivray, with the obituary from the *Edinburgh Messenger* the centre piece.

The clanking of cutlery brought Amy back to her present situation. She hurriedly closed the door, ran as silently as she could to the bathroom and flushed the toilet. She had barely made it back to the hall when Coates appeared. He looked suspicious, and Amy noticed his eyes flicking across to the closed door.

"You okay?" he asked, staring at the coat she had not taken off.

"Absolutely." Amy's voice was suddenly a little hoarse, and she cleared her throat. "I'm just feeling the cold."

"That's odd, you've gone quite red in the face," he observed without a smile.

"I hope I'm not coming down with something," she improvised.

"Well, there's nothing better for beating a bug than a bit of alcohol," Coates said, his tone light again. He ushered her into the living room where he had set up a tray with two glasses of wine and a plate with crackers and cheese.

"That looks delicious," Amy said, wondering if she should accept the glass Coates handed her. She couldn't help thinking how easily he might have hidden a colourless, tasteless liquid in it, and suddenly, she was scared. If she didn't take it, though, he would become even more suspicious.

"Cheers," he said, pinging his glass on hers and looking deep into her eyes. "To your new career."

He watched her as she slowly put the rim of the glass to her lips.

"Oh, I completely forgot," she exclaimed, putting the glass down before even taking a sip. "I haven't told my mum where I am. She'll be frantic with worry. Excuse me one second."

She pulled out her phone. On the screen she saw McCord's message and swiped it away. With trembling fingers, she scrolled down to his number, but a clammy hand suddenly clasped hers. The phone dropped to the floor.

"What's your game?" Coates hissed. "You sneak around my place and tell me a pack of lies. Who were you phoning?"

"My mum," Amy squealed. "Let go of me at once!"

The mace spray was uselessly sitting in her right pocket. There was no way she could reach it with her left hand. She kicked Coates in the shin, but instead of letting her go, he twisted her wrist and pushed her down onto the sofa, his heavy body right on top of her.

Amy opened her mouth to scream, but he put his free hand round her neck and squeezed until only a gurgling sound emanated from her.

"Women," he snarled with bared teeth, "you're all the same. Treating us like fools. But not anymore. You'll see who is on top now."

Amy felt his lower abdomen grind against hers as her lungs threatened to explode. With all the strength she had left, she swung her free left fist against his temple. Stunned, he loosened his grip round her neck for a second, enough for Amy to take a quick breath and take another swing, this time at his eye.

Howling with rage rather than pain, he grabbed a cushion and pressed it on her face. Amy fought back but was unable to move under her attacker's weight. Her legs kicked only air as little stars began to dance in front of her eyes.

That's it, she thought, I'm going to die. Her mum had told her about heaven when she was a little girl and how she would go there when she died. Will I need to ring a bell to get in? Amy wondered. I think the bell is ringing already. Please, God, let me in…

Suddenly, the pressure on her face and body eased, and she drew a couple of sweet, painful breaths. The stars dissipated, but the bell was still ringing furiously. Amy opened her eyes. Coates' distorted face was above her, his hand holding the cushion indecisively at his side. Somebody was hammering on the door.

"Open up, police!"

Amy recognised Calderwood's voice, and she cried out with relief.

Coates jumped up and threw the cushion across the room.

"You bitch!" he spat.

The hammering had ceased but someone was kicking against the cheap wood that sounded ready to give up.

"Stop! I'm coming!" shouted Coates.

To the sound of splintering wood, he rushed into the hall to let in McCord and Calderwood, whose leg was still poised in the air, prepared for another attempt at breaking down the door.

Without a word, McCord pushed both Calderwood and Coates aside and rushed into the living room. His eyes scanned Amy's dishevelled hair, the ashen, tear-stained face and her crumpled but intact clothes. His eyes sought hers, silently asking just one question. She gave him a nod and a weak smile, and he relaxed. Turning away from her, he pulled out his ID and addressed their reluctant host. He had been ushered into the living room by Calderwood, who looked ready to kill.

"Good evening, Mr Coates," McCord said, his voice only a menacing whisper, "DI McCord and DC Calderwood. We would like to have a word with you."

His orgiastic bout of violence having come to a premature end, Coates lowered himself onto the leather sofa that was still dented from Amy's body. Before he had even sat down properly, he began to spin a story in his defence.

"I'm the one who has been attacked here," he whined.

Amy nudged Calderwood and pointed to the door in the hall. Without hesitation, he followed her sign and opened the door. He stood still for a second, then he turned on the light in the cubbyhole and took pictures of the display.

When he joined the others in the lounge, McCord had already arrested Coates for aggravated assault and cautioned him. Coates sat with one hand covering his black eye, trying to look hard done by.

"Tell me," McCord was asking Coates, "about the messages you sent Martha McGillivray."

Coates seemed surprised at the direction of the questioning.

"I was drunk at the time, and upset," he explained. "I apologised to her afterwards, and she accepted it. I didn't mean anything I said."

"Really," Calderwood butted in.

He showed the picture of McGillivray's obituary amongst the other newspaper cuttings to McCord, whose eyes widened when he realised what he was being shown. Calderwood swivelled round and held the photo in front of Coates' face, which turned bright red.

"Care to explain your unusual tribute to Martha McGillivray in your broom cupboard?" Calderwood asked Coates.

"It is not illegal to keep newspaper cuttings," Coates blustered. "In any case, you had no right to burst into my flat without a warrant."

"We had every right to stop an assault, and quite possibly rape and murder," McCord countered. "We'd like you to accompany us to the station while our excellent forensic team see what other delights are to be found in your flat. You don't happen to have a chemistry set, do you?"

"A chemistry set? What's that supposed to mean? I haven't the faintest idea what you're talking about!" Coates shouted.

Amy had recovered her composure and was unable to keep quiet any longer.

"He knew that Martha died in great pain," she told McCord. "How does he know that? There was nothing in the papers about that."

"Indeed," McCord said with grim satisfaction. "DC Calderwood, handcuff Mr Coates and take him down to the car. I want to see what's in this cupboard."

He walked across the hall and inspected the shrine.

"What a nutcase," he muttered.

Then he turned on Amy who was rummaging through the kitchen looking for any signs of poison-making. "What were you thinking, going off with a guy like him?"

"I didn't know it was *that* bad," she defended herself. "If you hadn't cut me out of the investigation, I would have known what was going on!"

"Oh, I see – it's all my fault now, is it?" McCord's voice rose a few decibels with every word. "You went home with a man who you knew had written some horrible messages to a woman before. And why not have a glass of wine with a potential poisoner and wait to be raped or murdered!"

"Don't be so melodramatic," Amy said defiantly. "He's got a massive bruise on his temple and a black eye, and I still had this baby in reserve," she said pulling out the mace spray.

Amy knew, however, that he was right and that she ought to thank him for coming to her rescue, but the words stuck in her throat and refused to come out, so she followed him silently down to the car. At least, she would get into the station again now, and maybe Superintendent Gilchrist would realise how indispensable she was to the investigation.

On the drive back, Amy was in the front with McCord who wore a deep frown, while Calderwood sat next to Coates who only stopped protesting his innocence when Calderwood yanked the handcuffs painfully. After that, they made their way to the station in silence.

* * *

Fortunately, Gilchrist had left the building before McCord, Calderwood and Amy reached St Leonard's where McCord cautioned Coates again and formally interviewed him. Coates denied all wrongdoing apart from sending the messages to Martha McGillivray and claimed that Amy had attacked him after misinterpreting the pictures found in his broom cupboard. Asked how he knew about the manner of Martha McGillivray's death, he claimed that he had made it up to impress Amy. This was the only part of his statement McCord believed because if Coates had had a credible source, he would no doubt have made a splash of it in the *Messenger*.

Amy had made her official statement, in which she stressed the fact that she had suffered a serious assault and feared for her life when DI McCord and DC Calderwood arrived. Unfortunately, Coates with his bruised temple, an eye that was a purple swollen mess and a nasty cut on his cheek from Amy's opal ring, looked more the victim than the perpetrator. They also had no evidence regarding his involvement in Martha McGillivray's murder, so McCord, most reluctantly, had to let Coates go.

Afterwards, the three of them discussed the case in McCord's office exactly as they had in the past.

"So, we have five suspects, all of whom had motive and opportunity," Calderwood summarised. "Coates is clearly disturbed and capable of violence against women. Lomax and possibly the councillor had the strongest motive, and there is McGillivray's cryptic message pointing to Lomax, but neither he nor Councillor Weatherspoon seem like poisoners to me. Kirsty Hall and Zane Smith both had motive and ample opportunity. I suppose we need to search all their homes for chemistry sets and other possible evidence. We need warrants for all those," he said, turning to his boss.

"I've already applied for them," McCord said. "What makes matters so very difficult is that we need to check all their alibis for a time span of over thirty-five hours. That is almost impossible."

"You left out two other suspects," Amy said. "Whoever stole the laptop, unless it was one of the five, and the ex-husband, Shug McCain. Have you spoken to him yet?"

"He was not our top priority," McCord said defensively. "We've been rather busy recently, as you well know."

"Hall put me onto him," Amy said, "and she was right about Coates, wasn't she?"

McCord shrugged. "We don't know if Coates is the killer, but he is certainly a nasty piece of work. My guess is, now that McGillivray is dead, you are his new bête noire. I'm telling you, stay away from this case until we have something on Coates that can put him safely behind bars."

Amy did not even dignify this suggestion with an answer.

Calderwood picked up the pile of printouts. Thankfully, they were ordered according to sender and time, so it did not take him long to find the exchanges between McGillivray and Shug McCain.

"Hang on, let's see if he left any love messages for McGillivray on her phone."

There was an awkward silence between McCord and Amy while Calderwood was scanning the relevant pages.

"How is your mother?" McCord asked Amy eventually, just to say something.

"She's fine, thank you. The boutique is going very well. She had a dozen orders for a society wedding, so she is very busy."

"That's great. And John? All well at *Forth Write* magazine?"

"Fine, thanks. His mother has been kindness itself since Andrew, you know..." She fell silent.

McCord nodded, not keen to be reminded of the outcome of his last case. "Anything in those papers, Calderwood?"

"Not much," Calderwood muttered. "But then they only go back four weeks. There is one rather formal and polite exchange about the death of Shug's father only four weeks ago. Seems odd given how volatile their relationship was."

"I'll try to find out more," Amy offered. "Seeing that you have your hands full with the other suspects."

McCord looked as if he had swallowed a toad.

"I suppose so," he said eventually. "As long as you don't arrange to go home with him too. And as long as Gilchrist doesn't find out."

Amy smiled.

"He can't stop a journalist from investigating, can he. Besides, it is my citizen's duty to pass my findings on to the police, is it not? And whatever you tell me, he will never know."

McCord smiled back.

"It's getting late. You'd better leave, or it'll be difficult to explain to Superintendent Gilchrist why it took you over two hours to make a simple statement."

Chapter 14

The following day, Councillor Weatherspoon led McCord and Calderwood into a beautifully furnished living room with a bay window which overlooked a quiet, sunlit street lined with Victorian semis. His wife had rushed off to make some refreshments, so McCord came straight to the point.

"We're here in connection with Martha McGillivray's murder–"

"I thought you might come to see me," Weatherspoon interrupted him. "It's because of that blasted newspaper article, isn't it?"

"Not only because of that," McCord said. "Other evidence has emerged which points to a connection between the West Middleton project and Martha McGillivray's death."

The councillor eyed him expectantly, but McCord did not say more. It was always better to keep them guessing.

"That article contained nothing but speculation." Weatherspoon's easy smile had given way to a frown of moral indignation. "Yes, Godfrey Lomax is my son-in-law, but that had nothing to do with the awarding of the contract."

"It doesn't look good, though, does it?" McCord asked. "Are there no rules regarding conflict of interest?"

"There are very robust rules," Weatherspoon replied, "and they were followed to the letter. My connection to Godfrey was made clear to all who had a vote, and I actually abstained."

"After lobbying very hard for Lomax Construction for weeks," McCord said.

"They offered the best deal for the taxpayer, and they have a very good track record unlike the other bidders. Also, they're based in the Borders, which means work for local people. There are minutes of all the discussions which went on at council meetings. You don't have to take my word for this, you can read it all for yourselves."

"Oh, don't worry, we shall," McCord said.

He turned at a noise at the door. A few yards into the room stood a boy of about fifteen. He was wearing a maroon school uniform with white stripes that made him look like an entertainer on a nineteenth-century sea promenade. The only thing missing was the straw hat. Realising that his father had visitors, the boy hastily withdrew with a nicely worded apology.

"A very polite young man," Calderwood remarked, counteracting the bullish attitude McCord always employed with the upper echelons of society. "They do teach them good manners at those schools."

"Unfortunately, they are also very expensive," McCord added pointedly.

Weatherspoon was about to say something when his wife returned with a heavy tray. He jumped up to take it from her and put it carefully down on the coffee table.

"If you'll excuse me," Mrs Weatherspoon said to the detectives, "I need to give Thomas his lunch, he has a debating competition later on."

Clearly, it had never occurred to her that the police visit could have anything to do with her, and from the worried look on her husband's face McCord deduced that it might be better to speak to Weatherspoon on his own.

"Don't let us keep you," Calderwood said to Mrs Weatherspoon. "I'm sorry that we came at an inconvenient time."

McCord glared at him, but Mrs Weatherspoon smiled.

"Not at all. Please let me know if you need anything else."

In the hall, a girl's voice shouted, "Mum!"

"Coming, my darling!"

Mrs Weatherspoon hurried back to her maternal duties, and Weatherspoon visibly relaxed.

"I take it your wife doesn't know about your financial situation?" McCord asked.

Weatherspoon turned to the more sympathetic Calderwood.

"I don't think I have to disclose details about my finances, do I?"

"I'm afraid it has a bearing on the investigation," Calderwood explained, "and DI McCord has already applied for a warrant to access your accounts and search your property. This is going to happen later today."

"That's right," McCord said. "We also need a detailed account of your whereabouts from the evening of the thirteenth until the afternoon of the fifteenth. With witnesses if possible. It would be easier all round if you cooperated. The sooner we have all the facts, the sooner we can eliminate you from our inquiries."

"You don't seriously think that I had something to do with the death of that journalist?" Weatherspoon asked, aghast.

"We're ruling nothing out," McCord said coolly. "Can you confirm that you are in serious debt?"

"Nothing I can't deal with," Weatherspoon said defiantly. "A momentary shortfall."

"School fees for two are quite a drain," McCord said, "as is the upkeep of a house such as this, and I hear that you spend a lot of time on council business, which does not exactly pay well. If it is done legally," he added.

Weatherspoon opened his mouth to protest, but McCord carried on.

"The three-hundred-million-pound contract was quite a catch for Mr Lomax, and he might well have been prepared to show his appreciation for your help, if you get my drift. Martha McGillivray's activities could have led to a police investigation and cost him that contract, and cost you an opportunity to get yourself out of a tricky financial situation."

"That is not what happened!" Weatherspoon had raised his voice and now was looking nervously towards the door.

McCord waited until the councillor faced him again.

"Let's assume you have nothing to do with Martha McGillivray's death. Do you think Godfrey Lomax might have taken matters into his own hands?"

"This is crazy," Weatherspoon whispered. "Galashiels is not the Wild West. Godfrey and I are both involved in a project that will benefit the community as a whole, even if there are some people who are opposed to it. That is their right, but they cannot go about spreading lies about us and making us murder suspects! And now my whole life is being turned inside out!"

"I understand your frustration," Calderwood said. "The only thing you can do now is to be honest about all your dealings with Lomax Construction, and then we can hopefully bring this matter to a swift and satisfactory conclusion."

For us at least, McCord thought. Weatherspoon was very nervous about the investigation, and why would he be if he had nothing to hide?

* * *

"You're very quiet today, Amy," John remarked as they walked with Martin along George Street in a rare spell of winter sunshine towards their favourite café. "Your mum and I were wondering if you are not under shock from your ordeal yesterday and perhaps should have taken a day off at least."

She had not told them of her suspicion that somebody had been following her; she knew that if she did, Martin would never let her out of his sight and probably even follow her into the ladies', while John would try to forbid her going out altogether until he had hired a bodyguard. It was a cause of great frustration to her that she was unable to write about her horrific experience at Coates' flat until the legal proceedings and the McGillivray case were concluded and Coates turned out to be either McGillivray's killer or innocent. Whichever way it went, it could take weeks, or months at least.

"Nonsense," Amy rebutted John robustly, "I'm fine."

But she couldn't help glancing behind her as they turned into Frederick Street. Slipping one arm into John's and the other into Martin's, she told herself not to be silly. Why would anybody want to follow her?

* * *

Back at St Leonard's, PC Mike Turner had been waiting impatiently for his boss to return from his visit to Councillor Weatherspoon.

"It took me ages to check all the people who got onto the train with the victim at Galashiels, but I could not find any link to the case."

"PC Turner. Don't tell me what you *haven't* found. What *have* you found?" McCord asked.

"Him." The young officer proudly held up a mugshot. "Davie King. Already on our system for burglary and theft. He got on the train at Gorebridge without luggage and came off at Waverley carrying something that looks suspiciously like a laptop case."

"Excellent! Nice work."

He turned to PC Turner who was bouncing up and down on his heels.

"What are you waiting for? A gold star? Go and make your first arrest!"

"Yes, sir," PC Turner beamed, "but that is not the only interesting thing I found. I also checked the CCTV footage at Waverley on the morning of the day Martha McGillivray died. And guess who was there when the victim boarded the train."

Triumphantly, he held up a printout.

"I'll be damned," McCord said quietly. "You've just earned two gold stars, PC Turner. Now go and pick up Davie King."

The constable ran off. Calderwood was sitting on the edge of his chair.

"Who was the other person at the station?" he asked.

McCord turned the picture so that Calderwood could see it.

"Zane Smith!" Calderwood exclaimed.

"Who said that he was at home all the time," McCord added. "Bring him in."

* * *

Calderwood was barely out of the door when PC Dharwan announced that a Mrs Sandra Omerton was waiting in Interview Room 2.

"Shit! Already?" McCord muttered. He was keen to speak to Kirsty Hall's future mother-in-law, but he liked to prepare for interviews. In this case, though, he decided not to make the witness wait unnecessarily.

"Tell her I'm on my way."

Sandra Omerton was a pleasant-looking lady in her mid-fifties, McCord guessed. Dressed with unobtrusive elegance, she looked every inch the mother of a future prime minister. She accepted the abominable brew from the drinks machine that PC Dharwan had brought her as if she were being handed an Earl Grey from Harrods.

"Thank you very much for coming in to help us," McCord said. "We think you might have vital information regarding our investigation into Martha McGillivray's death."

Sandra Omerton tilted her head in surprise.

"Really? I have no idea how I can help, but please ask away."

"On the evening of 14th November, you were in the SKYbar with Kirsty Hall, your son's partner, to celebrate the news of her pregnancy, is that right?"

"That is absolutely correct," Sandra Omerton said. "Unfortunately, my son Charles was unable to join us because he was held up in his surgery. He is so conscientious, his constituents always come first."

"Do you remember a lady talking to Kirsty while you were there?"

"The journalist Kirsty was friendly with? Yes, she was also there with a male friend."

"That was Martha McGillivray," McCord said.

"Dear God! The woman who was killed on the train at Waverley? I did not realise that."

Sandra Omerton looked shocked. McCord wondered why Kirsty Hall had not told her about the connection.

McCord thought carefully about his next question. It was important not to lead a witness but to let them tell you what they actually saw rather than confirming what you wanted them to have seen.

"Could you tell me exactly what happened at the SKYbar? Every tiny detail could be important."

He motioned to PC Dharwan, who had her notebook ready.

Sandra Omerton stroked an imaginary crease out of her skirt.

"Well, when Kirsty arrived at the bar – I was there before her – I ordered champagne to toast the baby. Kirsty said no to my offer because of the alcohol but I told her I had a tiny glass when my husband and I found out that I was pregnant with our Charles, and it never did him any harm, Charles I mean, not my husband."

She beamed at the mention of her son, but then her face clouded over. "Sadly, my husband died soon after Charles was born, and he never got to see him grow up."

"I'm sorry, that must have been difficult for you," McCord said, barely hiding his impatience.

He needed to get her back on track.

"What happened then at the SKYbar?"

Sandra Omerton stared at the wall, as if trying to visualise the scene.

"I had forgotten to order any snacks, and Kirsty said she was hungry and needed a strong base for the champagne, so I went up to the bar and ordered a sharing platter, you know, cheese and olives and such like. When I came back to the table, the waiter had poured us each a glass. Kirsty said she needed the toilet – that happens when you're pregnant, you know – and I thought it was bad timing because the champagne would go flat. But Kirsty was back in a minute. We were about to have our drink at long last when that lady – Martha, was it? – came in. They greeted each other, and Kirsty said, we should all have a drink, so I went over to the bar to get two more glasses. By the time I got back, Martha had drunk one of the glasses already, and the waiter was refilling her glass. How rude was that? I was quite annoyed at the time, seeing that fine champagne being gulped down by people who were strangers to me as if it was mere juice and, after all, it was meant for our very special occasion. But if I had known what would happen to that woman the very next day, I wouldn't have grudged her a whole bottle, poor dear."

She paused, throwing a glance at PC Dharwan, who was scribbling away furiously.

"Are you sure you want to know all this?" she asked McCord.

"Absolutely," he assured her. "What did Martha do then?"

"She said something to Kirsty about giving back the key to her flat, and then she nodded to me, didn't even bother to make conversation–" Mrs Omerton hesitated, obviously realising she was criticising a murder victim "–and then she went over to their table with her companion, a good-looking, younger man. He seemed embarrassed at her behaviour and said something, but she just laughed."

"Did you observe what they were doing after that?" McCord asked.

Sandra Omerton's eyes lingered again on the bare wall that seemed to be a canvas for her memories.

"They ordered drinks and talked," she said eventually.

McCord hesitated, but then he asked the question.

"Did you see the man add anything to Martha's drink?"

Sandra Omerton looked at him wide-eyed.

"You think he may have poisoned her?"

"We don't know that, and I must ask you not to speak to anybody about this," McCord urged her. "It is only one of many possibilities we are investigating."

Sandra Omerton shook her head.

"I couldn't say. Martha was sitting with her back to us and obstructed the view of the man. And anyway, Kirsty and I were busy talking baby matters."

McCord sat quietly for a moment.

"Did you have the impression that Kirsty knew that Martha would be there?" he asked.

Sandra Omerton looked confused as if she did not understand the relevance.

"I don't know. Come to think of it, neither of them said the usual things one would say, like 'fancy seeing you here' or words to that effect. I asked Kirsty who that woman was, and she said she was a colleague she used to work closely with, but not anymore."

McCord thought about this for a moment before he continued, "Who left first, you and Kirsty or Martha and her companion?"

"We did," Sandra Omerton said without hesitation. "Kirsty said she was quite tired, which is natural of course. After all, it is hard work, being pregnant."

"I'm sure you're right," McCord said, having no experience with pregnancies whatsoever. "Many thanks, Mrs Omerton. I think that's all for now, but if you can think of anything else that might be relevant, please call me."

He handed over his card and accompanied her to the door.

When he returned, PC Dharwan handed him her notes.

"Nothing definite, is there?" she said.

McCord slapped his thigh in frustration.

"It confirms what the waiters said. They didn't see anything suspicious either, but they had also noticed that Kirsty Hall went to the toilet during her stay in the SKYbar, and Sandra Omerton did say that she spent some time at the bar, which means she would not necessarily have seen what the others were doing. So, all we know is that both Smith and Hall could have poisoned McGillivray that evening."

Chapter 15

Amy had spent an hour outside the flat where Shug McCain rented a room. She kept ringing the bell, but there was no answer. Her feet were numb with the cold, but at least it was dry. In Edinburgh in November, one had to be grateful for small mercies.

Amy had no particular desire to run into Shug McCain in the dark, nor to walk home on her own after sundown, for that matter. The incident with Cameron Coates had shaken her more than she admitted to anybody else, and she still could not rid herself of the feeling that someone was watching her, although any time she quickly looked behind her, she could not see anybody who suddenly turned away and slunk into dark doorways. 'You're being paranoid,' she scolded herself, stomping her feet as if all this was the pavement's fault.

She was about to give up on Shug McCain when the entrance to the flats opened to reveal an old woman who looked harmless enough. With her sunniest smile, Amy approached her slowly so as not to alarm her.

"Excuse me," she said, "do you know where Shug McCain is? I was supposed to meet him here, but he is not answering the door."

"You must have got your times wrong, dear," the old lady croaked, "Shug is always in the pub round the corner at this time most afternoons, drowning his sorrows."

"That is sad," Amy said. "Is he still not over the divorce?"

The old lady eyed her suspiciously.

"Who did you say you were?"

"I'm his great-niece," Amy improvised, "over from Australia for a couple of weeks. Discovering my roots," she added for good measure.

"That's funny," the old lady said without a smile, "he has never once mentioned he has relations from down under, and you don't sound like an Aussie. I could have sworn you are pure Edinburgh."

She looked Amy up and down as if she was committing every detail of her appearance to her fading memory.

"My mum always insisted we spoke proper," Amy ventured, feeling she was on dangerous ground here. "Thanks anyway, bye."

She hurried off in the general direction where the woman had pointed, hoping she would find the pub with Shug inside before the neighbour could tell him all about the strange great-niece that did not exist.

When Amy turned the corner, there was not one pub, but three in her line of vision. She started with the first one, a grim place straight out of a 70s movie where the only punters were two men with arms like tree trunks and tattooed necks. Hearing the door creak, they put down their pool cues and stared at her. A seamless hundred-and-eighty-degree turn saw her back out in the street and walking towards the next one along the road.

This one was a lot more inviting with gold lettering over the entrance and a board outside advertising live music. Light spilled out onto the pavement through the windows, and she was greeted with laughter and the cheerful clink of glasses when she pushed open the heavy wooden door. The place was fairly busy, even at this early hour, and Amy was relieved to see quite a few women among the drinkers.

Amy scanned the bar for a face that resembled the latest picture she had in her possession of McGillivray's ex-husband. It was from five years ago and showed a curiously square face with dark blue eyes under bushy eyebrows. She was about to leave and try the third establishment, when a man in a grey beard turned his head and looked straight at her. The untamed facial growth softened the sharp angles around the jawline, but it was definitely Shug McCain. Being in a public place emboldened Amy to take the direct approach. She got herself a glass of white wine from the bar and walked up to his table.

"Is it okay if I sit here?" she asked, pointing at the unoccupied chair.

"Please yourself," Shug McCain answered, although his tone and demeanour were not exactly inviting.

He took a sip of his bitter without taking his eyes off her. Feeling slightly uncomfortable under his scrutiny, she made an attempt at small talk.

"Do you come here often?"

"If you want something, spit it out," McCain said instead of an answer. "No, let me guess. Press. Not the big guns. Something niche but just about lowbrow enough to be tickled by a murder and other people's dirty linen. You want to ask me about Martha McGillivray, don't you? The usual questions – what was she like? And more importantly, what was our marriage like? And even more invasive, what was our divorce like? How am I doing? You probably even wonder if I killed her. Oh yes, I know your type very well indeed!"

He had raised his voice, and the punters around them had fallen silent and were listening. Amy put on a brave smile.

"You are a very perceptive man, Mr McCain. My readers would be very interested to hear your side of the story. After all, there are some not very nice things being said about you."

"Are there now."

Shug McCain stood up, which did not make much difference to his overall height, but he was still taller than Amy and about twice as broad. His squat, fleshy frame exuded strength, and his voice was far from friendly.

"If you had done your homework, girl, you'd know that I am a journalist myself, so if I wanted to read anything about myself in the papers, I would write it myself, you…"

A string of varied, vulgar expletives followed, and Amy was about to withdraw in humiliation when a tall young man in a baseball cap, who had been unable to keep his eyes off Amy since she had come in, squeezed between her and McCain.

"Oi, that's no way to talk to a lady. You should be glad if someone wants to hear your pathetic little life story. And come to think of it, some of us in here have actually been wondering why the polis haven't been in already to talk to you about your ex's murder–"

What else the young man might have wanted to say was drowned in a wave of Belhaven Best that hit him right in the face, soaking his Hibs cap and the front of his shirt. Not having a pint in his hand with which to retaliate, he instead punched McCain in the face, whose nose spurted blood so liberally that within seconds his face and jumper were dyed as red as his opponent's were brown. With a howl of rage, McCain threw himself at his foe, knocking him down to the floor along with Amy who had been standing behind him.

Arms were eventually stretched out to pull her out from under the two men who were pummelling away at each other. The landlord pleaded for an end to the violence, but two factions had formed in the pub, one in support of McCain and one for the young man evidently called Ewan, who was egged on by their shouts of, "Get him, Ewan, knock the hell out of him!"

The landlord made another attempt at peace-making, but it soon became obvious that it would be in vain. Resigned, he called the police and stood by while his pub was being trashed.

* * *

One and a half hours later, after giving her statement to the police, Amy left the pub, limping with a twisted knee that had been trapped under the weight of the two fighting men, both of whom had been arrested for causing an affray and damage to property. With tears in her eyes, she called a taxi to take her home. She would definitely not be mentioning this incident to McCord, or to anybody else for that matter.

Chapter 16

"Nice to see you, Russell," Keith McCord greeted his son when he arrived with the second curry of the week. "Are you staying over tonight?"

"I was hoping to," McCord said. "I could murder a pint or two."

In truth, whenever McCord had managed to put the case aside, he had been thinking about his dad's strange behaviour and decided that he ought to get to the bottom of it.

"Great. There is something I want to talk to you about," his father said, clasping and unclasping his hands.

Here we go, McCord thought.

They were silent until they sat down at the small table in the living room, their fragrant curry in front of them.

"Okay, Dad," McCord said, unable to bear the tension any longer. "Spit it out."

Keith sighed and put down his fork.

"See the trophy?"

"Yes, for winning the bowling competition. You showed it to me last time," McCord said, beginning to worry about an early onset of dementia.

"It was funny," Keith continued, "the lady who does the engraving wasn't sure how to spell McCord, with or without the 'a', as in Mac or Mc, and a big or small 'c'."

"Yes?" McCord muttered, seriously concerned now. His father had never been prone to havering before.

"Well, Clare, that's her name, phoned me up about it and we ended up having a nice chat."

McCord prayed to a God he did not believe in, that his dad would not recount the conversation word for word, which old people always seemed to do.

"Anyway," Keith ploughed on, "it turned out that we both enjoy going to the cinema, so we arranged to do that a few days later."

Suddenly, it dawned on McCord where this conversation was going.

"You mean you went on a date with that woman?"

"Well," Keith hesitated, watching his son's face closely, "I wouldn't call it a date, but we enjoyed each other's company and we've been doing things together since then."

"Doing things together?" McCord echoed, incredulous. "You mean, this Clare is your *girlfriend*?"

"Well," Keith said again before taking the plunge, "I guess you could say that."

McCord's eyes automatically fastened on the picture of his mother on the mantlepiece. She had always been the only woman for his dad, in life and in death.

"It doesn't mean that I have forgotten your mother," Keith said, also looking at the photograph. "I will always love and miss her. But life is too short to be without love, and I've wasted far too much of it pining for a past that won't come back. And I have the strangest feeling that your mother would be pleased for me. She loved me, you know, and she would want me to be happy. I only hope at some point you might bring yourself to feel the same way."

A sudden fear came over McCord, a fear of losing these easy curry nights, of being able to drop in at the shortest notice and have a chat with the only person in the world who loved him without limit or condition.

Don't be infantile, he scolded himself. Your father should not be sitting at home waiting for you to pop in when it suits you. He deserves and needs a partner.

"I *am* happy for you, Dad," he said trying to look it. "It's just a bit of a shock."

Keith beamed.

"You'll like her. She's kind and clever and funny and very attractive, too."

His enthusiasm was infectious, and McCord could not help but smile. Then the detective in him stirred.

"Was she here before I came last time? You didn't turf her out, did you?"

Keith chuckled.

"We thought it better to prepare you before you meet her. She was very understanding. That's why I hid the trophy as well, until I was ready to tell you. But do eat your curry, it's getting cold."

"What does Clare do?" McCord asked, tucking into his lamb bhuna.

"She runs the little jewellery shop in the High Street. If you're okay with it, I'll invite her round for a meal sometime."

"That'd be great. I'd love to meet her," McCord lied.

Keith looked hugely relieved.

"But now tell me about what's going on with you, Russell. Are you getting anywhere with that murder case?"

"We're making progress, but it's a slow grind. It seems Martha McGillivray, the journalist who was killed, annoyed everybody she had dealings with. One of her fellow journalists was stalking and threatening her, and when Amy Thornton found out, he attacked her."

Keith dropped his fork.

"He attacked your Amy? Oh, my God!"

"She's not *my* Amy, Dad. The silly woman actually went into his flat with him, alone. Can you believe it?"

"Is she okay?" Keith asked, horrified.

"Calderwood and I arrived in the nick of time. He'll probably be charged with assault. Although, to be fair, he came off worse in the end. But it could have ended quite differently. She never listens, you know? I had explicitly told her not to get involved."

Keith looked shrewdly at his son.

"Personally, I think the pair of you are too little involved. Why don't you ask Amy out at long last? It seems to me, admittedly from a distance, that you've been dancing around each other for months now."

"Not so much Torvill and Dean as Ali versus Frazier," McCord said. "We quarrel most of the time. No, I really don't think she's interested in me."

"During the past year, she seems to have been at the station an awful lot for someone who's not interested," Keith observed.

"She's only interested in our work, always hoping for a story for her magazine. And even if that wasn't all, why would she be interested in me? She's got the likes of Calderwood wrapped round her little finger."

"Not that I am an expert in women," Keith said, "but I think they prefer men who are stronger than those they can wrap around their little finger. You should tell her how you feel."

"And make things awkward between us?" McCord exclaimed. "No way."

"Correct me if I'm wrong, but things seem to be awkward between you already. Has she not given you any sign of encouragement?"

McCord thought of Amy's arms round his back, her body against his and her lips on his cheek when he was at her flat during the Rock Killer case.

"She might have done," he conceded. "I'm not sure."

"Then maybe you should take the initiative, son?"

McCord hated these conversations that had become ever more frequent.

"Let's set up the chessboard," he said. "I want revenge for the other night."

Chapter 17

There are days when the universe grows tired of endlessly expanding and picks out one unfortunate individual to have its sport with. On those days, the best plan of action for this individual is to remain either in bed or on the sofa and to venture no further than the kitchen to retrieve food whose preparation does not require the use of any knives or other potentially dangerous implements.

Unfortunately, McCord did not recognise the signs. When he tripped over his slippers in the morning, he blamed himself for leaving them in the middle of the bedroom floor. When he cut himself shaving, he cursed the new blade he had just put in.

To further lull him into a false sense of security, the journey into work was uneventful as crawling into the city centre in the nose-to-tail traffic made accidents improbable unless one fell asleep at the wheel or finally succumbed to a fit of violent road rage. Hence, McCord was quite unprepared for what the day had in store for him.

When he arrived at the station, he decided to tidy up some paperwork that was not only cluttering up his desk but also his mind. As he bent forward to feed some sheets containing sensitive information into the shredder, his tie was caught in the counter blades and slowly but relentlessly disappeared inside. Frantically, he pulled on it, but the shredder refused to let it go.

Choking now, he fell to his knees and fumbled for the off switch. Eventually, the whining of the rotor stopped, but McCord was still trapped in this ignominious situation when Calderwood's concerned voice sounded above him.

"Are you all right, sir?"

"Stop asking stupid questions and get the bloody scissors," McCord growled.

Calderwood swiftly executed the order and freed his boss from his entrapment. McCord loosened the knot and stood up, trying to look casual, while brushing some dust off his knees. With danger to life and limb averted, both men stared at the savaged neckwear, McCord in furious disbelief, Calderwood barely suppressing a grin.

"Maybe if I cut the end to give it a symmetrical point, then it might look almost–"

"I'll do it myself," McCord snarled, snatching the scissors from his partner. The slithery material made cutting a straight line nigh well impossible, and the edges began to fray immediately, but before McCord had a chance to utter the oath that was hovering on his lips, there was a knock on the open door.

"Superintendent Gilchrist wants to see you, sir," PC Dharwan said, glancing at McCord's tie, the scissors in his hand and the shredder at his feet. Without batting an eyelid or a change in the tone of her voice, she continued, "He would like an update on the case."

McCord had no doubt that she had fully grasped the situation and understood that a comment was not welcome. He was equally sure that she would not gossip about it with the other officers.

"Thank you, PC Dharwan," he mumbled, meaning more than her delivering the message.

Gilchrist was busy signing papers when McCord entered his office, and kept him waiting for a while, just long enough to establish who was boss. When he looked up, a frown clouded his photogenic face.

"You look a mess, DI McCord. Or is this a new fashion trend that I have missed?"

"No, sir," McCord said, quietly fuming, "I had a little mishap earlier."

Gilchrist showed neither sympathy nor glee, he only sighed.

"Where are we with the McGillivray case? Speculation is rife in the press that we are looking for a poisoner, and apparently one of the more popular questions asked on google is how to prepare ricin at home. If we don't catch this killer soon, we might have a whole spate of copycat killings on our hands."

On *my* hands, McCord thought, but aloud he said, "We are doing our best, sir."

Gilchrist looked sceptical. "Was anything found in the homes of Godfrey Lomax and Councillor Weatherspoon?"

"No," McCord had to admit.

"Anything unusual in their accounts? Suspiciously large transfers, cash withdrawals?"

"No, sir."

"But surely, the thief who stole the laptop has been apprehended by now?"

McCord had the distinct feeling that Gilchrist, despite his apparent concern at the lack of progress, was secretly enjoying himself.

"No, sir, but PC Turner is watching his flat and has been there all night. He is determined to make his first arrest and he declined my offer to have him relieved at midnight. He is a very promising young officer."

He did not want to tell Gilchrist of his fear that King had done a runner or was lying dead in a ditch somewhere.

"When PC Turner brings him in, we might find out what happened to the laptop.

"That is not an awful lot, is it, DI McCord."

"No, sir."

And with that, McCord was dismissed and returned to his office, more inclined to murder Gilchrist than to find the killer of Martha McGillivray.

McCord stared at her last message. Why had she been so sure it was Lomax? DC Sutton had found nothing regarding the West Middleton project on the USB stick that Kirsty Hall had handed over. Maybe Hall had been lying, and McGillivray had kept some additional information on the laptop.

"Sir?" PC Dharwan interrupted McCord's gloomy thoughts.

He looked up hopefully.

"Please tell me you've got some good news, PC Dharwan."

Suspiciously, he watched her put down a little cardboard tray with a barista-made coffee from the café next door and a lemon muffin. Everybody at the station knew it was his favourite.

PC Dharwan hesitated.

"It's news but not necessarily good news. It might not be relevant, but I felt you should–"

"Come on, let's have it," McCord said wearily.

Gently, she laid the front page of the *Edinburgh Messenger* on his desk, next to the coffee.

'PUB TRASHED IN JOURNALIST BRAWL' the headline told the readers, with a page full of pictures illustrating the story. One showed the pub looking like a war zone. In another, which was a little squint and had clearly been taken on a mobile phone, McCord could make out a squat man lying on top of a taller and thinner man with his arm raised, ready to thump him. Sticking out from under the fighting pair was a small figure with a face that was familiar, even though it was distorted in terror, a face with an unmistakeable nose. Another picture showed Amy leaving the pub, her hair a mess and dragging her left leg.

"Sorry," PC Dharwan said when McCord groaned softly. "The guy on top is Shug McCain, the ex-husband of Martha McGillivray. He's still at Gayfield police station. Apparently, he assaulted a police officer during his arrest and spent the night in a cell. I thought you'd want to speak to him, but maybe after you've had a little break."

McCord looked up at the bright young officer who should, if there was any justice in the world, go far in the force, but the 'Thank you' he wanted to say refused to come out.

PC Dharwan gave him a knowing smile.

"You're welcome."

* * *

Amy had taken a taxi to work that morning because her knee was still swollen and painful. Martin had been aghast at the sight of it and immediately fetched the cushion he usually sat on and placed it on a chair so she could put up her injured leg.

"Thank you," Amy said, planting a kiss on his rouged, bony cheek.

"What happened?" John asked gently, and Amy was relieved that her ignominy had remained a private matter.

"I fell awkwardly and twisted my knee," she said, assuaging her conscience that this was, strictly speaking, not a lie.

"Yes, those pub floors can be very slippery, can't they?" John put the front page of the *Messenger* on the desk in front of her.

Amy turned crimson, while Martin yelped with fright.

"How on earth did you end up underneath *two* men?" he asked.

"No need to be jealous, Martin."

But John did not smile. "What happened in that pub, Amy?"

128

Amy, realising there was no wriggling out of this, told the whole story, not even attempting to paint herself in a favourable light.

"You couldn't have known that those Neanderthals would start a fistfight simply because you asked a few perfectly sensible questions," Martin came to her defence before John could even say a word. He turned to his boss and oldest friend. "Look what those brutes did to her!"

"I can see that clearly," John said with a deep frown. "And that is why I'm asking you, Amy, to step back from this so-called police work and concentrate on the job you are actually paid for, which is writing human interest stories for this magazine. I appreciate that your coverage of DI McCord's cases has done wonders for our circulation in the past, but you have been in serious danger and hurt twice now in the course of two days."

Amy was about to protest, but John held up his hands, clearly determined to be heard out.

"I fear your mum is going to kill me, or worse, split up with me, if there is another incident like this. You will now be concentrating on the article about Charles Omerton, so that it is ready for publication for next Saturday's edition. As for you, Martin, I hold you personally responsible for making sure that Amy, for the time being at least, avoids all possible contact with any potential murderers."

"I'm not going to be told where to go and who to speak to," Amy bristled. "But don't worry," she added in a more subdued tone, rubbing her throbbing knee, "I'm not going anywhere in a hurry with my leg like this."

John and Martin gave a simultaneous sigh of relief.

"Let's find out what kind of man this Charles Omerton is." Amy turned her mind back to work. "You never know, if he really becomes First Minister or even Prime Minister, and he needs friendly press coverage, we will want to be the paper he turns to, won't we?"

Amy had just unlocked the screen when her phone rang. McCord. Maybe this was about something else?

"How's your leg?"

Damn.

"Absolutely fine," she said with clenched teeth.

McCord cleared his throat.

"How do you know?" she asked, silently praying that at least he had only heard rumours and not seen the humiliating pictures.

"You are on the front cover of this morning's *Messenger*," McCord said, dashing her hopes, his voice now loud and clear. And angry. "Didn't I tell you to stay away from this case? One day you'll get seriously hurt playing detective. I'm of a mind to have a protection officer follow you around, but sadly, Gilchrist won't stand for that." His voice became a little lighter. "And since every interview you conduct ends in arrests for all sorts of offences apart from the murder we are investigating, can I suggest that you leave it to me and Calderwood to interview suspects from now on? Police Scotland are running out of available cells."

Amy made a very unladylike sound. "Ach, bugger off, McCord."

She heard him laugh as she furiously stabbed the red icon.

Chapter 18

McCord was secretly pleased to see the damage done to Shug McCain's face. His broken nose had been set but was still swollen and blue, matching the dark blue tissue surrounding the narrow slit where his right eye used to be. An attempt had been made to clean him up, but little flecks of dried blood added a dash of colour to his greying beard, and his jumper sported a large maroon stain across his broad chest.

"Maybe this little incident will teach you not to be rude to a lady, Mr McCain," McCord said after he had introduced himself.

"What do you want?" McCain asked wearily.

Any anger McCain might have harboured seemed to have been drained from him during his night in a cell. "I've made a statement admitting to all the charges, and I'll pay for some of the damage as long as the other fellow does as well. After all, he started the fight."

"I'm a homicide detective. I'm not interested in pub brawls," McCord said. "Our clever IT people have retrieved the messages you sent to your ex-wife going back six months. Some of them bear a striking resemblance to the language used last night. We've also heard from your neighbours that during your marriage you more than once caused a disturbance, and only Ms McGillivray's intervention stopped them from calling the police."

"Damn busybodies," McCain muttered. "Just because nothing is going on in their married life, they're meddling in other people's."

"They said they were concerned for Ms McGillivray's safety."

McCain snorted. "There was no need. And what about my safety? Martha gave as good as she got. Most of the flying crockery they might have heard smashing was flung by *her* at *me.* Believe it or not, I loved that woman, still do and probably always will."

"You must have been bitter about the divorce then?" McCord asked.

"It had become inevitable. Martha only did things on her terms. If she was fed up with you, you went."

"Why was she fed up with you?"

McCain thought for a moment. "The hunt for a really good story was all that ultimately mattered to Martha. Did you know we were in Kosovo together and in Darfur?"

McCord nodded and waited for McCain to continue.

"Well, if truth be told, what we witnessed there, really sickened me. I used to come back to our room, exhausted but unable to sleep. Martha was the opposite. She only came truly to life when she was in the thick of the action, no matter how bloody or terrible it was."

McCain rubbed his eyes as if trying to erase the pictures imprinted on them but winced as he touched the swelling.

"There came a point when I had had enough of it. We were filming and reporting atrocities so that people here could watch while having their tea, shaking their heads, saying how awful it was, and then carrying on exactly as before. I became more and more angry about it all and refused to go with her to war zones. Martha saw that as a betrayal, as weakness. Whatever she had felt for me, it died within her. And after the statutory one-year separation, we divorced."

"But she had retired – if that's the right name for it – to Edinburgh in recent years herself, hadn't she?"

McCain smiled ruefully.

"She was not as young as she felt anymore. Running away from shelling while carrying a rucksack and a twenty-pound camera is a young person's game, especially when you don't have the backup of a big organisation. But she missed the action, the adrenaline rush, and it made her very grumpy. I think she blamed me for the lack of excitement. I was like a chain round her neck, she once said."

The last sentence was barely audible.

"Did she ever tell you what she was investigating since coming back to Edinburgh?" McCord asked.

"She gave the impression that she was about to bring the whole establishment down, but I think she was only trying to rekindle the excitement of the past," McCain said, having recovered his normal voice. "She was very secretive about her stories. She might have shared some of her plans with that young woman – Kirsty Hall, she was called. Treated her a bit like the daughter she never had, her professional heir."

McCord nodded. "She put Hall in her will, but then planned to cut her out just before she died – do you have any idea why she would have done that?"

"No idea," McCain said. "We've hardly had any contact since the divorce came through."

"Do you know anything about her relationship with Zane Smith?"

It was difficult to gauge this man's feelings behind the beard and the bruises.

"She only took up with him after we split up," McCain said. "If you ask me, she was going through some form of midlife crisis. Going about with a much younger man maybe made her feel young again. He's some sort of model, isn't he? I don't know, never met the guy, and she never talked about him."

McCord decided to change tack.

"The divorce settlement was not exactly in your favour, was it? You must feel hard done by."

McCain looked up, surprised.

"Money was never an issue. While we were married, we shared what we earned, and Martha brought in a lot more money than me. She had the knack of getting people to tell her things, and she was a bloody good writer. When we divorced last month, she kept the flat she had inherited from her parents, and we split the rest. I've put a bid in for a nice place in Queensferry."

"Still, reading your texts one could hardly call the divorce amicable," McCord argued.

McCain gave a laugh, bitter and nostalgic at the same time.

"Even our marriage was never *amicable*," he told McCord. "It was fire or ice, passion or war. Martha didn't do warm and cuddly. But she was one hell of a woman." He hesitated. "Can I ask you a question?"

Surprised, McCord nodded.

"What happened to your tie?"

"An altercation with a shredder."

McCain grinned. "I sympathise. But even that is not as scary as a woman yielding scissors. One of Martha's finest moments. The journalist in the pub was right, I really should tell my side of the story."

McCain agreed to write down where he was during the thirty hours leading up to McGillivray's death. As he said himself, there was nothing else for him to do while he was sitting around in a cell. McCord had lost his appetite to persecute the man further. If asked to place a bet on one of the two men in McGillivray's life being the killer, his money was still on Zane Smith.

Chapter 19

Like a fox terrier with a rabbit, PC Turner dragged his prey into St Leonard's and presented it proudly to his master.

After a sleepless night and nearly twenty hours in his car, PC Turner had finally made his first arrest. Davie King had done a spot of burgling and then spent a satisfying night at his girlfriend's. When he had returned in the morning, he found an overtired and very bad-tempered PC Turner waiting for him, who arrested him on the spot and demanded to see the contents of his bag. Even a man like Davie King, to whom lying had become second nature, had difficulty explaining the provenance of the lady's jewellery, iPod and golden cigarette case which the police officer pulled out of his bag.

McCord gave due praise and asked PC Turner to join him during the interrogation. Having been caught red-handed, King was already fairly pliable when McCord and PC Turner entered Interview Room 1.

"Right, Davie," McCord began. He tended to be equally polite – or rude in some cases – to suspects as he was to witnesses unless they had been convicted of a felony before. After repeated contact with known individuals, he felt entitled to a certain familiarity and first-name terms. "We've got you for burglary, so let's not waste time on that. What we are *really* interested in, Davie, is the laptop you nicked from the Galashiels train on November 15th and offered to the editor of the *Edinburgh Messenger* for two thousand quid."

"A laptop? November 15th?" Davie King repeated as if McCord had been telling him about the underlying principles of string theory.

"Maybe you get confused, Davie, with all the stuff you steal in a week, but I'd like you to think back to that day when you walked through the first-class carriage of the Galashiels to Edinburgh train and lifted a laptop bag, which is understandable because nobody was paying attention to it, and besides, it really suits you."

McCord slapped a print of the CCTV image from Waverley on the table.

King's eyes darted from one detective to the other, as if the appropriate lie could be found in their faces, or perhaps he was looking for some sign which might reveal who was the more gullible of the two. Then he saw McCord's tie and was so mesmerised by it that he seemed to have forgotten why he was there in the first place.

Angrily, McCord stuffed the lower half of the remaining tie between the buttons of his shirt. That seemed to break the spell, and King looked up, attempting another delay to his answer. "A laptop?"

"Let me help you out here, Davie," McCord said in a tone as if he was speaking to a child. "This laptop belonged to a lady who was murdered. She died on that train, minutes before you lifted her laptop. We think that the laptop contains vital information and was possibly the reason why she was killed. So, don't you worry about any charges of burglary. It's more likely to be murder or, at the very least, accessory to murder."

McCord observed with satisfaction how the blood drained out of Davie King's face.

"However," McCord continued, his voice now sharp, "if you tell us who put you up to this and where the laptop is now, we might be able to keep your sentence to under ten years." He leaned back in his chair. "I'm listening, Davie."

"I didn't kill nobody!" King shouted. "I had no idea who it belonged to, and I only found out she was dead when I watched the news later. I was just shuffling along, and there it was, sitting on the table, and nobody around, so I took it. I swear that's the truth!"

"So, where is the laptop?" McCord asked, leaning forward.

Davie King bit his lip.

"Where is it, goddammit?!" McCord shouted.

"I chucked it," King said quietly.

"You what?" McCord banged the table with his fist. "Don't lie to me. A seasoned wheeler-dealer like you doesn't throw away an expensive piece of kit like that. Who did you sell it to?"

"I didn't sell it to nobody," King whined. "Well, I tried to sell it to that newspaper guy, but when that went wrong, and there were polis all over the place, I got the heebie-jeebies. I was scared, I tell you. I didn't want to be caught up in a murder case, and what with everybody looking for the laptop, I didn't dare shift it. I couldn't get into it either, the security on it was ridiculous, so I took a hammer to it and threw the pieces in a bin a few streets away."

McCord closed his eyes in despair.

"It didn't occur to you to hand the laptop in anonymously after you heard that it was important to a murder inquiry?" PC Turner stepped in.

"Yes," King said, quite earnestly, "but then I thought you guys are so clever with your forensics that you'd probably find out it was me who took it, so I figured it was best if it disappeared altogether."

McCord groaned.

"Take him to his cell, PC Turner, before I throttle him. Then go home and catch up on the sleep you've missed. And, by the way, well done."

* * *

"How did it go with Davie King?" Calderwood asked expectantly when McCord returned to the office.

"You won't believe it," McCord fumed. "The moronic, pea-brained half-wit smashed the laptop to pieces when he realised it was connected to a murder inquiry and it would be impossible to sell. I'll add concealment and destruction of vital evidence to his charge sheet, as well as criminal idiocy. When I think of all the manhours spent on trying to find that laptop!"

"Well, thank God we have the USB stick," Calderwood said, "so it wasn't such a loss in the end."

"If Hall has indeed told us the truth, but I doubt that," McCord said. "It would not surprise me at all if she has copied some of the information for herself and deleted it before handing in the stick. The other thing we do know is that McGillivray no longer trusted her. Why else would she want her flat key back? We will need to bring Hall back in for another little chat. She is involved in this, I am sure."

"You might want to speak to our toy boy first, though," Calderwood suggested. "I brought him in while you were interviewing King. Maybe the laptop is immaterial after all if Zane Smith is our killer. He's in Interview Room 2 right now."

* * *

Zane Smith had dark rings under his eyes, and despite a liberal dash of aftershave his skin was sallow. He was immaculately dressed and carried a small leather bag. McCord could not help but notice his not only intact but also tasteful tie and briefly wondered if he could arrest Smith and take it away as a potential suicide risk.

"Is this going to take long?" Smith asked McCord. "I have an audition at eleven that I really need to attend."

"I can imagine that you are pressed for funds," McCord answered coolly, "and Martha McGillivray's estate can't be dissolved until the investigation into her death is complete. Which would happen more quickly," he added, "if you had not made a false statement. But then again, if you are convicted of her murder, you will not inherit at all, so it must have seemed a risk worth taking."

Whatever colour had been left in Smith's face now disappeared out of it. He looked the personification of guilt. McCord turned over the sheet in front of him and revealed the CCTV still showing Smith at Waverley Station five minutes before McGillivray boarded the Galashiels train.

"Care to elaborate?" McCord asked.

"I... I..." Smith covered his face with his palms and began to sob.

McCord glanced over to Calderwood, who shrugged. There was no telling whether Smith was acting or not.

"At this point," McCord said calmly, "we have you eating and drinking with Martha McGillivray at the SKYbar, which is well within the time frame she could have been poisoned. We also have evidence of you following her to the station where she boards the train on which she dies. You could have got on the train, followed her to Galashiels and poisoned her. You probably came back on another train to make sure you were not linked to her murder. We have not yet checked all the CCTV coverage at Waverley and Galashiels that day, but we will if we have to. The longer you make us spend on this, however, the less well intentioned we will be towards you."

McCord leaned forward.

"If you confess now and give us your side of the story, the court might consider being lenient. But if you persist in lying to me, I for one will do my best to get you behind bars for the rest of your miserable little life."

Smith lifted his head, tears glistening in his eyes.

"I didn't kill her!" he shouted.

"If you didn't, what were you doing at Waverley that morning?" McCord demanded.

Smith pulled a freshly ironed hankie out of his trouser pocket and blew his nose.

"I followed Martha to see where she was going," he said, staring at the wall past McCord. "At the SKYbar the night before, I didn't poison her, I proposed to her. I can show you the ring if you like."

McCord tried to keep a straight face. Was this guy deluded or a pathological liar?

Calderwood, in contrast, looked intrigued.

"How did Martha react to your proposal of marriage?" he asked.

Smith bit his lower lip.

"She laughed in my face. Then she said she was sorry but that it was never going to happen and that it might be better if we broke up."

"That must have come as a shock," Calderwood sympathised.

"Do you think?" Smith laughed bitterly. "I begged her to reconsider, but she told me to man up and face reality."

McCord flicked through the file.

"The waiters at the bar didn't notice any such drama," he said.

"I didn't make a scene if that's what you think," Smith bristled. "I was bitterly disappointed, in denial even, and still thought she was making a huge mistake. I couldn't believe she was dumping me."

"But you did leave the SKYbar together?" McCord insisted.

"Martha paid and left, and I followed her outside. She called a taxi and went off. When I got home, I phoned her. She said there was nothing to talk about, that it was over. She told me that she was not feeling well, anyway, so could I leave her in peace and let her get on with her life."

"But instead, you started stalking her," McCord observed.

"I didn't *stalk* her," Smith shouted, "I loved her! I was worried about her because she had been so secretive about her investigations and because she said she was not well. Martha was never ill, all the time I knew her. She had the constitution of an ox."

Smith smiled ruefully.

"Maybe you also wondered if she had another lover," McCord suggested. "Someone she was meeting in Galashiels?"

"The thought had crossed my mind," Smith admitted. "That morning, I wanted to follow her onto the train and try to talk to her, but then I chickened out. I can't help thinking that I might have saved her if I'd got on that train with her..."

He buried his face in his hands again.

McCord and Calderwood looked at each other, clearly thinking the same: they were not going to get a confession to McGillivray's murder from Smith today, and they had no way of disproving his story unless they found CCTV of him somewhere between Edinburgh and Galashiels on that very day.

"You can go off to your audition now," McCord said, grimly. "But we may have to talk to you again. Please don't leave Edinburgh without telling us."

"Thank you."

Zane Smith shot out of his seat and was out of the door in less time than it took Calderwood to switch off the recorder.

"What do you think?" Calderwood asked McCord.

"He *could* be telling the truth, I suppose. What I do find interesting is that he remembers McGillivray saying she wasn't feeling well later that night."

"You mean that she was poisoned that day, maybe in the SKYbar..." Calderwood's voice trailed off.

"By Kirsty Hall," McCord finished the sentence.

"But then why the message warning Kirsty about Lomax?" Calderwood asked.

"Maybe McGillivray didn't make that link. She suspected Lomax of all kinds of evil and when she realised that she had been poisoned, she naturally assumed it happened at Lomax Construction where she had been a couple of hours before, and she knew that Kirsty still had her key and would publish the story."

"But if she was already unwell the evening before? Would she not have wondered if she had been poisoned then? Hold on." Calderwood flicked through his notebook. "She only had water at Lomax's office, the secretary said. And on the train, she had some more water and the crackers from the bakery." He looked up at his boss. "Which would fit in with someone who is not feeling great."

"Maybe she was on a diet and wasn't sick at all," said McCord, "and she told Smith that to get him off her back. But you've made a good point. We need to dig deeper into the involvement of Kirsty Hall."

Chapter 20

"Is everything okay, Martin?" John Campbell asked anxiously, when he came back early to the magazine offices after a meeting had been cancelled at the last minute.

His political editor was clad in brown corduroy trousers and a cream-coloured jumper accessorized with a matching scarf, and he was sliding his arm into a fawn-coloured raincoat.

"Of– of course," Martin stammered, "why should anything be the matter?"

"You have never worn anything like... *this* in all the years I have known you. Are you sure you are quite well? You know I am always here if you need someone to talk to. Have you been feeling depressed lately?"

"Not at all," Martin hastily reassured his old friend, "but I really need to go now."

"Where to? Do you have a meeting with the 'powers of beige'?" John asked, his grin masking his concern.

"It's just that Amy..." Martin faltered.

John Campbell sighed.

"Why am I not surprised that this strange get-up you are wearing has something to do with our Amy? What on earth is that girl up to now?"

"Nothing, she says she has the feeling that somebody is following her, and she wants to catch him at it. So, she asked me to walk behind her in an unobtrusive manner to see if I can spot him tailing her."

John Campbell had turned pale.

"Somebody is following Amy?! And instead of calling DI McCord, you play the amateur sleuth in that ridiculous outfit?"

Then he saw the hurt in his old friend's eyes.

"I am sorry, Martin. I did not mean that to sound as it did. What matters now is: where is Amy?"

"I'm right here," said Amy, who had witnessed the whole conversation from behind a half-open door and now stepped into the room.

"I'm sorry, Amy," Martin wailed, "I know John wasn't supposed to know..."

"It's okay." She turned to John. "I didn't want to worry you."

"I always worry about you, so let's go and catch who is following you," John said grimly, putting his coat back on. "And then we'll take whoever it is to DI McCord."

* * *

Amy was walking slowly and with a slight limp along George Street towards St Andrew Square. A fresh wind was blowing the different layers of clouds into swirls of white, grey, and purple, their rims turning golden whenever the low sun hit them.

Don't look back, she kept telling herself. She felt silly, dragging John and Martin out on such a cloak-and-dagger operation, just because of a gut feeling. It wasn't always there, but she seemed unable to shake it off or to convince herself that she was only imagining things.

The truth of the matter was that she was scared to travel out to Fife on her own to interview Charles Omerton, and being scared was not a state of mind she relished, nor was she used to it. This had to stop, one way or the other. If John and Martin did not notice anybody, she would accept that her fear was simply an overreaction to the bad experiences she'd had in the past few days, but if they did, they would put an end to this creepy game of hide-and-seek.

As arranged with John and Martin, she stopped at the window of a shop selling fabrics as if she had found something of interest in the display, and then stepped into the shop. Anybody loitering outside would be quite conspicuous, they had thought, as there were not normally many pedestrians on this stretch of the road. Inside the shop, she smiled at the lady behind the till who was rushing forward to serve her.

"Just browsing, thank you," Amy said and turned round quickly to glance out of the window. All she could see was a woman pushing a pram with one hand while dragging a toddler along with the other.

Under the watchful eyes of the shop assistant, Amy pretended to be interested in the beautifully embroidered curtain fabrics and cheerful rolls of waxed tablecloth.

"Wonderful stuff you've got," she said, sincerely, "but stupidly I've left the note with my measurements at home. I'll be back another time."

As she stepped out into the road, she gave a start as she found herself right next to Martin and John, who had cornered an ostensibly outraged Cameron Coates.

"You will get out of my way immediately," Coates blustered. "This constitutes assault and is wrongful deprivation of my personal liberty. I'm going to call the police!"

"There is no need," Amy said. "I'll call DI McCord right away. I'm sure he'll be very interested to hear that you have now been stalking me in addition to the charge of assaulting me in your flat."

She took a photo of him next to the fabric shop as evidence.

"I took several photos of him on the way," Martin said proudly. "He can't wriggle out of this one."

Amy clicked on McCord's name, and he answered immediately.

"Everything okay?"

"Never better," Amy said. "I've got Cameron Coates here who has been stalking me for the past few days, which also explains the photographs taken in the pub. John and Martin are going to bring him into St Leonard's station now."

There was a deep intake of breath at the other end.

"Okay. See you in a few minutes then."

"I'm off to Cupar, actually," Amy said. "I've got an appointment there. But I think I'll be quite safe travelling on my own now."

* * *

McCord thoroughly enjoyed formally arresting Cameron Coates again. Faced with the photographic evidence combined with John's and Martin's witness statements, Coates had no choice but to admit to stalking Amy. Taken together with the previous assault on her and Coates' threatening messages to Martha McGillivray, McCord was able to compile a report that would result in at least a restraining order and possibly even a prison sentence.

"Well, thank you very much," McCord said to Martin and John after Coates had been led away to be processed for a few overnight stays. "I'm very relieved that this headcase is out of circulation for a while."

John nodded seriously.

"I have told Amy to stay away from police business," he said, "but she simply will not listen."

"That's because she's so very good at it," Martin cooed, his eyes glazing over. "She knew she was being followed, and it was her who had the *brilliant* idea to catch Coates *in flagrante*."

John shook his head.

"What if he had not been there today but the next time when she was on her own?" he said. "What if he had attacked her in some dark alleyway when we were not there to protect her? She has been attacked *twice* in the past three days!"

McCord held up a hand. "To be fair, Shug McCain didn't actually attack her. I think she was unlucky to be caught up in the brawl. But I see your point entirely. She has an uncanny ability to attract trouble wherever she goes."

Martin smiled knowingly.

"And I can imagine how worried you must be each time she goes off on her own," he said suggestively to McCord. "You should keep her close, no matter what your Superintendent says."

McCord had had enough of Martin's matchmaking efforts for the day and stood up.

"I'm afraid, I need to get back to work. As much as I detest this fellow, Coates, I don't think he is our poisoner, so we still have to identify and catch a killer, after all."

John rose swiftly from his chair, clearly embarrassed to have kept the detective from more pressing matters.

"Thank you for looking after Amy – as much as she will allow it," he said to McCord.

"Why is she travelling over to Cupar anyway?" McCord asked. "Please tell me she is not pursuing another suspect!"

"Oh no," Martin hastily reassured the detective, "she is going to interview Charles Omerton, the MSP. No connection to Martha McGillivray at all."

"Well," McCord said, "praise the Lord for that."

Chapter 21

John had insisted on booking a first-class ticket to Cupar for Amy, and she had not argued. By the time the train approached the crossing over the Firth of Forth, she had already typed a few questions she was going to put to Charles Omerton.

When the train slowed down, Amy looked out of the window and, as always, was mesmerised by the view of three impressive bridges spanning the distance between Fife and West Lothian. Ahead of her lay the iconic red structure of the Forth Rail Bridge that was once synonymous with Sisyphean tasks; once the painters had reached the end of the bridge, it was time to start again at the beginning. Nowadays, the paint used lasts twenty years, so people can admire the UNESCO World Heritage Site without it being marred by scaffolding. The two road bridges, each a pinnacle of engineering in the century of their construction, rose to her left, blinking in the intermittent sunshine. With the railway line being over a hundred metres above the water, Amy had fine views of the naval dockyards at Rosyth and, from the windows on the other side of the train, the islands of Inchgarvie and Inchcolm, where numerous seabirds were circling. That had her fondly thinking of DI McCord and of how he would have enjoyed pointing out the various species to her.

When the train entered the small tunnel on the Fife side, she returned to her laptop, and by the time she was leaving the carriage in Cupar, she felt she had a good grasp of how she was going to conduct the interview.

A taxi, pre-booked by the ever-considerate John, was waiting at Cupar Station, and soon she was being greeted by Omerton.

"Thank you for seeing me, Mr Omerton," Amy said, shaking a warm, firm hand.

"Charles, please." North Fife's youngest ever MSP smiled. "Take a seat."

Noticing her bandaged knee, he solicitously fetched a second chair so that she could rest her leg.

Martin had been right. Charles Omerton certainly qualified for the term 'dishy', and his suit, although off the shelf as Amy immediately saw, set off his tall, slim frame perfectly. On the desk, Amy spotted a photograph of him with an attractive older woman who she guessed was his mother, and one of him and Kirsty Hall on a sandy beach.

"I must admit," Omerton said, "I am slightly puzzled by the interest *Forth Write* magazine is showing in me. First your colleague and now you. Not that I am not delighted," he added gallantly. "Mr Eden's cartoons are superb if not exactly complimentary about the Conservative and Unionist Party. He gave me quite a grilling on policy details, and I have a strong suspicion that he is a left-wing liberal."

"And you are quite right," Amy said, "but then our boss is a bit of a blue badge holder, as well as his best friend, so there is a good balance of political views at the magazine. We're not so much about party politics as about the truth and the best course of action for the Scottish people."

"Well spoken, Amy. You should be a politician yourself. And which side are you on?"

"None, really," Amy replied. "It's my job to be interested in people and I'm generally nosey."

Charles Omerton laughed.

"Well, I hope I can satisfy your curiosity." He spread his arms in an inviting gesture. "What would you like to know?"

Amy took out her notebook.

"How, having been privately educated, are you going to convince working class people that you have their interests at heart?"

"I wasn't born with a silver spoon in my mouth, if that's what you think," Omerton said. "My mother was a teacher, and my father died when I was very young. Money was tight, but my mother always fostered my thirst for knowledge and respect for education. I was extremely lucky to gain a full scholarship to St Nicodemus'. The headmaster, Mr Billington, who sadly is retired now, is a great man. He made it his mission to instil in his pupils a sense of gratitude and responsibility that should come with privilege. He really believed in the school's motto: *Hic servire* – Here to serve. I think it would be madness to dismantle organisations that provide an excellent education for the sake of equality; what we need is to make sure that every child in the country has access to the very best education. Don't you agree?"

Amy had been taking some notes, and now looked up.

"This idea has been touted before, but as yet the educational gap between rich and poor remains," she said. "From what Martin told me about your politics, you seem to be closer to Labour or the Lib Dems on many issues, so how would you define Conservative?"

"My idea of conservatism is quite simple and what it was meant to be originally. One: every individual's right to pursue his or her happiness as long as nobody else gets hurt, and two: to conserve what is good and improve what is bad."

"I imagine that would appeal to younger voters, but the majority of Conservative voters are older and will not be impressed with your modern ideas, will they?"

Omerton shrugged.

"Well, I can only do what I think is right. And the Conservative Party has not exactly done well in Scotland in the past decades, has it? Hopefully, the country is ready for a change."

"Word is that you have set your sights beyond Holyrood, on Westminster. Do you really think you are going to be Prime Minister one day?"

Omerton opened his hands in a non-committal gesture.

"If you study my speeches, you'll find that I have never expressed such an ambition. Some people seem to expect me to pack my bags ready to challenge the PM at the next election. For now, I'm proud to be serving as MSP for North Fife, and hopefully, if I do a good job here, the voters will entrust me with a greater responsibility one day."

Amy recognised a well-practised spiel when she heard one and decided not to make it too easy for Omerton.

"Are you going to face your responsibility toward your girlfriend as well? Having a child out of wedlock is not exactly advertising the family values of the Conservatives, is it?"

Omerton's smile became less radiant.

"I sometimes wish Kirsty would not be quite so forthcoming with details from our private life, but there we are. I'm not ashamed of it. Having grown up without a father, I'm very keen to have a family, and to be a good father to my child."

Amy did not say anything for a couple seconds, and her face must have betrayed her feelings at his words because Omerton asked quietly, "Am I right in thinking that your own family situation is complicated?"

Amy looked him in the eyes and sighed.

"I grew up without a father, too," she said, "but I don't even know who he is."

Omerton nodded in acknowledgement that hers was an aggravated case of being fatherless.

"I'm sorry," he said. "Somehow, there's always that huge gap in one's life, isn't there?"

Amy smiled, embarrassed at having given away so much of herself.

"Listen to me. Here I am, bothering you with my private affairs when I am supposed to interview *you*. So, what does Charles Omerton do when he doesn't do politics?"

"I've always been interested in science and inventions," he said, readily accepting the turn the conversation had taken. "I even tried to create a device that automatically turns pages in a book, a proper book I mean."

"I thought that already exists," Amy said. "It's called a licked finger."

Omerton laughed again.

"And what do you do to keep fit?" Amy asked.

"Badminton twice a week," he said, "and taking the stairs instead of the lift."

After another twenty minutes of pleasant chat, Amy left, utterly charmed and with the feeling that she might have voted for him at the next election, had she lived in his constituency. It was only when she was sitting on the train taking her back to Edinburgh that her journalistic instinct kicked in. This Charles Omerton seemed too good to be true. Tomorrow, she would pay his old headmaster a visit and see what he had to say about his prodigy. But what gnawed at her more than anything she had heard in this interview was one sentence: 'there's always that huge gap in one's life'. It certainly had been for her, and it wasn't just that someone had always been missing from her life; a part of herself eluded her, floated like an anchorless raft in a sea of possibilities.

Tonight, she would pluck up the courage to do what she had wanted to do all her life but never dared to – she would ask her mum about her father.

Chapter 22

McCord and Calderwood were sharing thoughts and comparing notes on progress made so far with the McGillivray case, when the office phone rang.

"DI McCord? There's a lady here, a Mrs Samantha Lomax, asking to speak to you," the duty sergeant told McCord. "She says you'll know what it's about."

"Thanks, Jack," McCord replied. "DC Calderwood is on his way to collect her."

Calderwood left, and McCord hastily removed what was left of his tie and undid the top button of is shirt. He decided that it was better to be casually complete than formally mutilated, especially when dealing with upper-class ladies.

A few moments later, Calderwood was ushering in the wife of Godfrey Lomax. She exhibited the confident bearing and stylish clothes of the privately educated and she greeted McCord without any sign of nervousness. As she took her seat, McCord could not fail to notice how the faint sunlight through the office window gave her ash-blonde hair a translucent sheen, almost as if she had a halo around her.

McCord, guessing that she was not much older than thirty, tried to picture her as Godfrey Lomax's wife, a vision that refused to form in his mind.

"Thank you for seeing me so quickly," Samantha Lomax said after introductions had been made and they had all sat down. "You must be terribly busy, but I think I might be able to save you some time."

McCord was intrigued.

"Fire away, Mrs Lomax."

"Samantha, please. My father, Councillor Weatherspoon, and my husband, Godfrey Lomax, have told me about your visits. They said that you insinuated that they are involved in corruption and possibly even in the murder of this poor journalist who died on the train. Is it true that your people were looking for signs of ricin production?"

She giggled, not nervously at all, but rather at the sheer incongruity of the very notion.

McCord could already hear Gilchrist thundering at him about antagonising the pillars of Edinburgh society.

"With respect, Mrs Lomax, we are not insinuating anything; we are merely following different leads in an inquiry. I'm afraid uncomfortable questions are always a part of that," he said, sounding more defensive than he had intended.

"Oh, I perfectly understand your point of view," Samantha Lomax said pleasantly. "My father had told me about Martha McGillivray before; she seems to have had quite an obsession with the West Middleton project, and it is only natural that you'd take her suspicions seriously. After all, you have a job to do. But I'd hate to see you wasting valuable time and resources on silly notions which will get you nowhere."

She took a sip of the station coffee, and for a split second, her pretty, expertly made-up face contorted in disgust. She put the cup down again.

"Oh, yes?" McCord asked. He just loved people telling him how to do his job, especially when he suspected that they had never done what he considered a full day's work themselves.

"What you don't know, DI McCord, but I can tell you, is that this is a dead end. My husband, God bless him, is a very successful businessman, but he doesn't have five standard grades to rub together. He was one of those who only come into their own when they leave school. He can't even boil an egg, let alone concoct a poison. He is also not a man who is overly concerned by hostility to his business plans. 'Dogs pissing on a tree', he calls that."

She laughed at McCord's puzzled look. "I get that a lot. The princess and the ogre. As a matter of fact, Godfrey is a very sweet and attentive husband, and we can't help who we fall in love with, can we?"

McCord wondered why a delicate, bronzed face with an aquiline nose sprang to mind, but pushed the thought aside.

"And as for my father," Samantha Lomax continued, "he is a long-serving and well-respected councillor – or at least was until the *Edinburgh Messenger* published that vile article – and definitely not a criminal mastermind either. He thinks the family has no idea about his money problems, but I've known for a while. In fact, I have spoken to my uncle, who is also my godfather and happens to be very comfortably off, and I persuaded him to contribute to my younger siblings' education. Dad has also remortgaged some of the house, so everything is under control. He doesn't want my mum to know, which is probably a good idea; she is such a worrier, and that knowledge would affect not only her peace of mind, but her general health. And anyway, Dad would be far too scared of being caught to even contemplate anything illegal."

Samantha Lomax had finished and looked expectantly at the detectives waiting for confirmation that her mission was accomplished.

"Well, thank you very much for coming in, Mrs Lomax, eh, Samantha," McCord said. "That was very helpful indeed. DC Calderwood, would you show our visitor out?"

* * *

When Calderwood returned, McCord was sitting at his desk in his thinking position, his face resting on his joined palms as if he was praying.

"Interesting," he said. "Which one of them sent her on this rescue mission, do you think? Lomax or Weatherspoon?"

"She might have come of her own accord," Calderwood replied. "She's the type who would take matters into her own hands if she thought it necessary. And she doesn't seem to have a very high opinion of either her father's or her husband's intellectual capacity."

"Exactly," McCord said. "So, she tries to throw us off the scent. Which makes us think what?"

"That we were on the right track, after all," Calderwood finished the sentence.

McCord nodded.

"It's back to Lomax. McGillivray must have had something else on him. She could have put it on her laptop the day she died but that is lost now, thanks to that obstacle to evolution Davie King. PC Dharwan has been through all the files on the USB stick and found nothing. Our only chance is Kirsty Hall. She could have transferred and deleted some of the files before handing it over to us. She had plenty time to do that. This is her first big break, and she would be extremely reluctant to give it up."

Calderwood smiled. "But luckily, we have somebody who can find any file there is, don't we?"

"Indeed."

McCord paid PC Dharwan a visit at her desk to pick up the USB stick and see what progress she and PC Turner were making tracing the whereabouts of McGillivray and their main suspects during the thirty hours before her death. Their strained and frustrated expressions told him the answer. PC Turner had found no sign of Zane Smith being anywhere near the victim after her train had left for Galashiels, and they had not broken anybody's alibi yet.

"Keep at it," McCord urged them. "We might get a breakthrough soon, but until then, we have to keep an open mind and follow all the leads."

* * *

McCord's knocks on DC Sutton's filing cupboard elicited no response. He knocked again, and then entered her den. She was not there.

"Where is DC Sutton?" he asked loudly, concerned rather than annoyed, in the general direction of the other staff working in the open-plan office. It occurred to him that he had never seen DC Sutton anywhere else but at her desk apart from his first day back.

"Here, sir," a croaky voice sounded behind him.

DC Sutton came from the direction of the ladies', clearly mortified at being the centre of attention.

"Sorry," McCord said, now embarrassed himself. "It's not that I object to you having a... break, I was just... worried."

She looked at him with her huge eyes, clearly mystified by the enigma that were other people.

McCord handed her the USB stick and moved aside to let her pass.

"I need you to recover any deleted files. Can you do that?"

She nodded, puzzled at this incredibly stupid question.

"Of course, you can. Sorry," McCord continued, stumbling on. "See if you can find anything on it to do with Lomax and the West Middleton project."

Without any further comment or even acknowledgement, DC Sutton disappeared into her space.

Chapter 23

When McCord returned to his office, yet another visitor was waiting for him. The man was in his mid-twenties. His lobster-red skin was peeling on his nose, which led McCord to the conclusion that he must have been abroad recently; to be more precise, at least a thousand miles south of Edinburgh. His baggy olive-green trousers sported more pockets than an SAS soldier's, but the hunched shoulders and nervously twisting hands were not those of a warrior. His eyes briefly locked into McCord's, only to swivel away to the window, seemingly searching for the answer to how he should begin his tale.

"I'm DI McCord. Please have a seat. I understand you have information relevant to the death of Martha McGillivray?"

The young man hesitantly lowered himself onto the chair in front of McCord's desk. It was obvious that he was nervous.

"You told me earlier your name was Matt Branston, and also that you knew Martha McGillivray. What can you tell us about her?" Calderwood asked kindly.

"I didn't *know* her, really," the young man began, but fell silent again.

McCord felt the strong desire to shake Branston to speed up the process. "So, why don't you tell us how you met her and take it from there," he said.

Branston looked at the detectives in turn and eventually found the courage to speak.

"I was at one of the meetings about the West Middleton project in the village hall in North Middleton. One of the local Green Party members had explained the environmental impact the building of all these houses and roads would have, when Martha McGillivray stood up and told us that she had seen the EIA."

"What is the EIA when it's at home?" McCord asked, growing increasingly impatient.

"The Environmental Impact Assessment," Branston explained, seemingly disappointed at the low level of expertise displayed by the guardians of the law.

"Ah, that one," McCord remembered, embarrassed. "We looked into that, but it seems there is nothing in the area that warrants particular protection."

"But, you see," Branston said, "I know that there *is* something there."

McCord perked up. "You do?"

"The EIA doesn't only cover natural features, but also possible archaeological sites that are of interest. I'm a postgraduate archaeology student, and last year I did a thesis on Bronze Age settlements in Scotland. On one of our walks around Middleton a couple of months ago, my tutor told me that he had previously flown over this area and that he would bet a thousand quid that there was a Bronze Age settlement underneath. He was about to start digging when the farmer came along and told us to move on. We did nothing about it at the time, but when I heard about the plans for building in that area, I went to the meeting."

Branston ground to a halt.

"And that's when you spoke to Martha McGillivray?" Calderwood asked.

"Yes, at the end of the meeting I asked her what the EIA said about sites of archaeological significance, but she said, according to the report, there was none."

"Well, you had no evidence for your suspicion, did you?" McCord asked. "Maybe your tutor got it wrong; after all, he had only scanned the surface from a height."

"That is true," Branston admitted, "but he is an eminent authority in his field, and Bronze Age settlements leave very distinctive lines on the landscape. I told Martha about it, and she was so keen that she wanted to investigate the matter straightaway."

He ground to a halt again, and even McCord was becoming concerned about the archaeologist's blood supply to his fingers that had turned white.

"Don't worry," he said, "we are not interested in minor transgressions; we are trying to solve a murder."

"I– I don't think we broke the law," Branston stammered. "Martha said there was a right to roam in Scotland, and that was what we were going to do, along with a little bit of digging."

McCord and Calderwood exchanged a look.

"So, you and Martha went a-roaming in the area and dug up something?" McCord asked, suddenly bright-eyed.

"Yes," Branston admitted, "but at night – to avoid the farmer. He was carrying a gun the first time my colleague and I met him. I was not happy about Martha's plan; after all, I'm not exactly Indiana Jones but she said we had to find out, and this was the only way."

McCord tried not to smile. He could just imagine McGillivray reliving the good old days when she had been in the thick of it, and dragging the poor, frightened archaeologist along with her.

"And what did you find?" Calderwood asked.

Branston delved into one of the deep pockets on the side of his trousers and produced a little parcel. He carefully peeled off the brown tape holding it together and unwrapped the plastic, bubble wrap and, lastly, the cotton wool, revealing a cleaned potsherd and an oval metal object with an intricate geometric pattern.

"Pieces of pottery, even a brooch. Martha was so excited. 'We've got him!' she shouted. Then we heard dogs barking and ran for it."

"When was this?" McCord asked, leaning forward.

"The night of the 12th. I was scheduled to go to a dig in Italy the following day. Martha said she would inform the Scottish Government that the EIA had been falsified, but before that she 'wanted to put the wind up Lomax's backside'. That's what she said," he added lest the detectives should think he would ever say anything so rude. "I didn't know about Martha's death until I came back yesterday. When I heard that she was murdered, I couldn't help thinking that it might be connected to our find, and, to be honest, I am now feeling scared and unsure about what to do."

"You've done the right thing," Calderwood said. "Your information could be crucial to the solving of this crime."

"But do you think I could be in danger?" Branston asked. "What should I do now?"

Calderwood looked to his boss for an answer.

"I don't think you are in immediate danger, Mr Branston," McCord said. "It is very unlikely that Martha told anybody about this."

Branston did not seem convinced. "Maybe I'll go back to Tuscany for a while; they always need volunteers out there."

"Why not, if it makes you feel better," McCord said. "But please leave us your contact details in case we need to speak to you again."

He pushed a sheet of paper towards him, and Branston started writing down his phone number and email address.

"By the way," McCord said, "do you know a woman called Gill?"

Branston looked up, confused.

"Gill? I have an aunt in Cheshire called Gill, but I haven't seen her for years. Why?"

"Never mind."

McCord tried not to show his disappointment as he watched Branston finish writing.

"Thank you very much for coming in," McCord said. "DC Calderwood will see you out."

When Calderwood returned, McCord had already pulled the picture of Martha McGillivray's last words from the file.

"'Lo arch dig gill' – Lomax, archaeological dig. We've got him, Calderwood. But who the hell is this Gill?!"

* * *

Amy had never been so nervous in her whole life. She was pacing up and down the living room of her flat, while waiting for her mum to come upstairs after closing the boutique for the night. They had always been close, Valerie and her, and she could not have wished for a better mother. In primary school, however, Amy discovered that other children had a daddy, but when she asked her mum where he was, Valerie had always brushed the question aside. What did they need a daddy for, were they not the best team in the whole world? Little Amy had been flattered and had to agree that her mother was amazing as mums went. Any further attempt to bring up the subject had been shot down, and while Valerie was a loving and fiercely protective mother, she was not a pretty sight when in a rage.

As a teenager, Amy had understood that life could not have been easy for a young woman bringing up a child on her own and, knowing how hard her mum worked and what sacrifices she made for her, Amy did not want to seem ungrateful. But now the question of who her father was could no longer be pushed aside. Omerton had been right. Amy knew she would never feel complete without that piece of the puzzle that made up who she was.

After what had seemed an eternity, she heard her mother's steps outside the door. She now wished she had not drunk three gin and tonics to give her courage as her brain felt fuzzy and her emotions jumped from bravado to sheer terror and back every few seconds.

The door opened, and Valerie came in, dropping her handbag and coat on the sofa with a sigh.

"Sorry, I'm late. A customer, five minutes before closing time. She wanted to buy a dress that would make her look like Audrey Hepburn; tricky when you're built like a Russian tank."

Amy did not laugh.

"What's the matter?" Valerie asked, suddenly serious. "Has something happened?"

Amy shook her head vigorously but when she tried to hold still, somehow she could not stop.

"You've been at the gin," Valerie tried to make light of the situation. "Not nice. If you invite somebody for a drink, you wait for them to arrive before you get plastered yourself."

"Mum!" Amy shouted suddenly, in a brief moment of alcohol-fuelled courage. "Mum, I need to know who my father is."

"Ach, not that again," Valerie snapped, her face clouding over. "We've been over this umpteen times. It's always been you and me, and you could not have turned out better if you'd had ten fathers. Anyway, when you see most of the fathers around, we were better off without one."

"Maybe *you* were," Amy said, trying to be calm. "But you never asked *me.* I have a right to know who my father is, a legal right!"

"Don't start with the law," Valerie sneered. "Where was the law when your father abandoned us and left me to fend for myself?"

Amy moved close to her mother and took her hands.

"So, he left you? Why? Who was he?"

Valerie pulled her daughter into her arms and kissed the crown of her head.

"Believe me, it is better if you don't know."

But instead of snuggling into her mother's body as she would normally have done, Amy pushed Valerie away.

"Stop treating me like a child. I'm twenty-six years old!"

"Exactly," Valerie said. "You're a grown, beautiful woman. What do you need a father for now, for God's sake? Come on, pour me a gin and tell me about this Omerton guy you were interviewing today."

Amy crossed her arms.

"No. No, I won't. Either you tell me now, or you can get out and go to John's."

"Are you throwing me out of my own flat?" Valerie asked, open-mouthed.

"Ah, I was wondering when that would come up," Amy said. "Well, I can pay rent to somebody else in the town, if that's what you want!"

Valerie picked up her coat and bag. "I've had enough of this."

On the threshold, she hesitated as if she wanted to say something conciliatory, but only an irate 'For God's sake!' came out before she banged the door shut behind her.

Amy stood motionless and stared at the door – a symbol of the barrier between her mum and her that she had conjured up with her demand. She should have kept quiet, as she had done all the years until now. What had she achieved? A rift between herself and the person she was closest to, a gulf that might never be bridged. Her legs suddenly would not carry her weight anymore, and, sobbing loudly, she collapsed on the sofa.

Chapter 24

When McCord and Calderwood stepped into Godfrey Lomax's office the following morning, he was less welcoming than during their last visit.

"What can I do for you today, DI McCord?"

"We have dug up new evidence," McCord said, watching the businessman closely.

Lomax's face betrayed nothing.

"Evidence of what?" he asked, feigning indifference.

"Evidence of falsifying an EIA and concealing information that would put a stop to your whole project. For years," McCord added for emphasis.

"What?!" Lomax's face darkened. "What evidence? Don't tell me somebody has chucked some endangered dung beetle into a field and now claims it was there before?"

"No, on the contrary. Somebody took something out of the area that West Middleton is going to – or rather *was* – going to be built on. Archaeological evidence of a Bronze Age settlement that will take years to excavate."

Lomax sat completely still for a moment. Then he banged his fist on the desk.

"I don't believe it. It must have been planted by one of the idiots campaigning against the project. I knew they were obsessed, but I didn't think they would stoop this low."

"You should be flattered about all the attention," McCord said. "Martha McGillivray's last message seconds before she died was all about you. Lomax, archaeological dig, it said. Are you seriously trying to tell me that she didn't confront you with her findings the last time she came to see you?"

Lomax did not answer immediately. McCord suspected that he was weighing up what he could get away with.

"She was throwing wild accusations around as always," Lomax said eventually. "But she did not produce any proof. Where is the proof?"

"At the police station," McCord said.

Lomax leant forward in his swivel chair.

"Listen. I commissioned a reputable firm to conduct the EIA. If they messed up and overlooked something, it is their problem."

McCord shook his head.

"On the contrary, it is very much *your* problem. The discovery of a Bronze Age settlement will set your project back years. Bearing that in mind, is it not possible that you encouraged the surveyor to ignore any potential stumbling block and made sure that Martha McGillivray would not publicise her findings?"

"No, it is not!" Lomax shouted. "I knew nothing of any Bronze Age settlement, I did not bribe anybody, and I most certainly did not kill that journalist!"

"DC Calderwood has taken due note of that," McCord said, unflustered. "But maybe you can tell me who Gill is?"

Lomax took a while to process the question.

"Gill? I have no idea. What does this Gill have to do with anything?"

"She was mentioned in the same message about you and the archaeological dig. We are going to find out who she is sooner or later, but it might be better for you if you cooperate with us now."

Lomax stood up, suddenly calm.

"Next time you want to speak to me, make an appointment, so that I can have my lawyer present. Good day, detectives."

McCord and Calderwood also rose.

"No doubt, we'll speak again," McCord said. "Goodbye, Mr Lomax."

Once they had stepped into the cool air, McCord's phone pinged. It was a message from DC Sutton.

Files recovered. Nothing on Lomax.

McCord stamped his foot in frustration.

"McGillivray must have had all the stuff about the dig on her laptop, and that is gone," he said. "We have no way of proving that Lomax knew anything about the settlement before McGillivray told him or that he bribed the surveyor to change the EIA. Hang on."

He quickly typed a message.

"I've asked DC Sutton to trace Lomax's calls," he told Calderwood. "I bet he's calling somebody about this right now, and I want to know who that is."

Still deep in thought, McCord started the engine of his Juke, and the car made an indignant leap forward. Swearing profusely, McCord stepped on the clutch, shifted the gearstick and steered the car slowly out of the parking lot.

* * *

Hector Billington, retired headmaster of St Nicodemus Academy for Boys, was delighted to interrupt his *Times* crossword to entertain an attractive young lady who was keen to listen to him reminiscing about happy times. He insisted on making tea and even produced Amy's favourite biscuits, chocolate-coated Hobnobs.

"Surprisingly, one misses the hustle and bustle of a school," he said. "All these young people around keep one young. But then, there is also a lot of hassle, usually from over-ambitious parents or over-zealous politicians, and some staff who think they know best; all aspects which one does *not* miss."

His strange habit of talking about himself in the third person aside, his mind was sharp, and his watery pale blue eyes astute.

"Charles Omerton, oh yes," he finally came to the point after entertaining Amy with a string of anecdotes from his twenty-year tenure at St Nicodemus'. "Strange you should ask about him. Only a couple of weeks ago, another lady journalist came and wanted to know everything about Charles."

Amy perked up.

"Was that journalist called Martha McGillivray, by any chance?"

"It was indeed," Billington said, scrutinizing Amy over his spectacles. "When I asked her what her interest in him was, she was very evasive. Maybe you could enlighten me?"

"I have no idea why she would be interested in him," Amy said. "But you must have heard that she was murdered last week?"

Billington tilted his head in regret, his eyes betraying both wariness and curiosity. "There was an obituary in *The Sunday Times*. She seems to have been quite a lady."

Amy nodded.

"She was. What did she ask about specifically?"

"She seemed interested in Charles Omerton's political views," Billington told Amy. "Odd, really, I was thinking at the time, she could have figured them out merely by reading his speeches."

Billington poured them another cup. He was obviously one of those who believe cleaning a teapot lessens the flavour of the drink, but Amy did not want to appear rude and ask for a coffee. In her experience, it was better not to ask elderly tea drinkers to make coffee anyway.

"You don't think Charles had anything to do with that poor woman's murder?" Billington asked.

"Not at all," Amy replied. "My colleague and I are writing a feature for our magazine, seeing that he is the new poster boy for the Conservative Party and touted as a potential next leader."

"I can believe that," Billington said. "He always was ambitious."

"What was he like as a boy?"

The old headmaster chewed thoughtfully on his Hobnob before he answered.

"Bright, hard-working, well-behaved."

"Every teacher's dream then?" Amy asked.

"I suppose so. Never put a foot wrong. Great, of course, but sometimes I wished he had been just a little bit naughty. It almost seemed… unnatural."

Then a memory came to him that made him giggle.

"There was once when Charles' Latin teacher wrote in his report that he was 'inattentive and easily distracted'. The next day his mother was in, complaining and saying that surely it was the teacher's job to keep bright pupils like her son interested and to make sure that there were no distractions in the classroom."

"And what did you say to that?" Amy asked with a smile.

"That I would have a word with the teacher and with Charles, and that I was sure this would not happen again. It was more than my life's worth to antagonise Mrs Omerton although she never paid a penny for his education. Charles had a full scholarship, you know. Quite deservedly, I must say. Head Boy in sixth form and left with straight As. Debating champion three years in a row and a very promising scientist. Shame, really, that he should squander all that by going into politics."

Amy thought back to Martha McGillivray's visit.

"So, what were his political views as a teenager?" she asked.

"You know how they say if a sixteen-year-old is not a socialist, he has no heart?"

Amy shook her head and laughed.

"Well, he was a committed Conservative even when he was thirteen," Billington said. "I would never go as far as to say he had no heart, though. In fact, my staff and I never saw or heard him being unkind."

"Could it be that he was simply never caught?" Amy asked.

Billington pondered this.

"I suppose it is possible. But we knew our pupils very well. After all, it is the individual care and attention that the parents pay that little bit extra for."

"To the tune of £35,000 a year," Amy said.

Billington smiled.

"Money well spent, in my opinion, although, to be honest, Charles with his desire to succeed would probably have done well in any school. Maybe because he was so precocious and articulate, he seemed like a mini prime minister in school uniform even then."

After many more memories and stories, Amy thanked Mr Billington profusely and left him with a promise to drop in with a copy of the article when it was out.

* * *

Thankfully, there was a bus stop right outside the old headmaster's home. Amy was still unable to drive because her knee seized up when it was in the same position for too long. The next bus was due in ten minutes, so she pulled out her phone and tapped on McCord's name. He answered after the second ring.

"You okay?"

"Of course," Amy replied tetchily, "I don't *always* get involved in a citizen's arrest or a pub brawl when I'm out. Is Gilchrist around or is he tapping your phone?"

"To answer the first question, he isn't, thank God, and the second, I sincerely hope not. What's up?"

"I've just been to see Charles Omerton's headmaster."

There was a pause at the other end.

"Charles Omerton is Kirsty Hall's boyfriend," Amy prompted.

"Of course," McCord said. "What's he done?"

"Nothing. Martin and I are writing an article about him and his stellar rise in Scottish politics. But what might interest you: Martha McGillivray beat me to it. She was here two weeks ago, asking Omerton's former headmaster about his politics."

"Two weeks ago," McCord muttered.

"Too long before her death, and I doubt very much that Mr Billington is in the habit of poisoning people – although you never know, of course," Amy said with a giggle. "I do wonder what McGillivray was after. It would be typical of her to try and dig up dirt on a future party leader. Has there been any mention of Charles Omerton in the case?"

"Nothing, apart from the connection to Kirsty Hall. I suppose living in sin and producing illegitimate offspring ceased to be a reason for blackmail when Boris Johnson became prime minister. Did Omerton's former headmaster not have *anything* bad to say about him?"

"Nothing at all, which he himself thinks is odd. Charles seems to have been born with 'strait-laced Conservative' tattooed on his forehead."

"If Martha McGillivray had an interest in Charles Omerton, we need to take a closer look at him as well. Thanks," McCord said.

At that moment, a delightfully old-fashioned double-decker bus turned the corner at the end of the street.

"Bus is here. Have to go," Amy said. "Keep me posted."

"Will do. Take care."

He had hung up before she could berate him for patronising her.

* * *

Amy dragged herself up the steps to her flat as if she was carrying a heavy weight on her shoulders. Her knee was still swollen, and the lights were off in her mother's boutique. She must have closed the shop early and gone home. Home to John. Suddenly, Amy felt utterly alone. Maybe her mother was right, and she was behaving like a child, clinging on to a mother who had finally got her own life after devoting hers to bringing up her daughter, and a father who was only a phantom. It was time she built her own life.

As she tried to turn the key, she realized the door was unlocked. The lights were on in the hall, and Amy wondered if she had forgotten to switch them off before she left. Or could it be a burglar? Then she noticed her mother's coat on the hook next to the door.

Apprehensively, she entered the living room. Her mother sat at the table, a bottle of Amy's favourite gin, decorated with a huge bow, in front of her. Valerie pointed to the Caorunn.

"A peace offering," she said, quietly. "Can we talk?"

Amy dropped her bag and coat where it fell and sat down.

"I talked to John yesterday," Valerie began. "And he gave me quite a row."

Amy was so surprised that she laughed.

"John? Never. John's idea of a row is a polite question. And besides, he adores you."

"Inexplicably, yes," Valerie said. "But he made me see that I was wrong all those years, and ultimately selfish although I always told myself that I was only doing what was best for you." She looked at Amy pleadingly. "Is it really that important to you?"

Instead of a reply, Amy got up and hobbled across to her bedroom. Kneeling down beside her bed was excruciatingly painful, but with clenched teeth, she pulled out an old cardboard box from underneath and carried it into the living room.

"Open it," she told her mum.

Hesitantly, Valerie took off the lid. Letters, hundreds of letters, all addressed to 'Daddy' or 'Dad' or 'My Father'. Valerie picked up one after the other, recognising her daughter's handwriting as it had changed over the years.

With trembling fingers, she opened one addressed to 'Daddy'. It was full of questions: 'Where are you?' 'When are you coming to see me?' Another one said: 'To My Father'. Valerie tore it open. More questions. 'Who are you?' 'Who am I?'

All her life, Amy had written to a ghost, into a void.

"I am so, so sorry," Valerie whispered, tears streaming down her face.

"I have to know, Mum." Amy's voice shook.

Valerie nodded and picked up her handbag. She pulled out a brown A5 envelope and handed it to Amy.

"There," she said in a barely audible voice, "meet your father."

When Amy shook the envelope, a photograph and a folded sheet of paper fell out. She looked inside but this was all there was. First, she picked up the photograph. It showed a smiling couple in front of a French café. The woman was a very young, radiant Valerie, and she was leaning against a short, olive-skinned man in his thirties. It came as a shock to Amy to see her own features in a strange man's face.

"I was an au pair in Paris," Valerie explained. "He was a teacher at the college where I took French lessons."

Amy cleared her throat.

"What was he like?"

Valerie sat down heavily.

"Attractive, charming, clever. Good with words. Something you must have inherited from him. We spent a wonderful summer in Paris when I was there. I was in love with him and thought the magic would go on forever."

"What happened?" Amy asked.

"I found out I was pregnant. And that he was married. What a cliché."

As Amy put the photo down and reached for the letter, Valerie tried to snatch it from her.

"Leave it. It will only hurt you more. He had his own family and didn't want us. That is quite enough. Let it go."

But Amy was having none of it. She unfolded the plain white paper to reveal the only words she would ever have of her father. There were only a few lines in French. Vertical, straight and neat, they told Valerie that he naturally was not going to leave his wife and family and that having a child on her own now would not be right for her either, so here was the address of a discreet private clinic where everything would be taken care of. An appointment had been arranged and paid for since he was keen to do the right thing. 'Good luck and goodbye. Nicolas.'

Amy's hand sank slowly onto the rough surface of the table. It was scratched and scored from her mother's early work as a sewing lady to keep them both fed and clothed, discoloured from the crafts Amy did at primary school and bleached from many a hot cup of chocolate over which Amy had told her mum all about her woes and adventures. She dropped the letter and clutched her mother's hand.

"I am sorry, Mum," she said. "It must have been so hard for you."

Valerie stroked Amy's palm with her thumb, crying silently. "It was. But it got better all the time, and I was so happy to have you. I should have given you the photograph ages ago and burnt the damn letter. I suppose it kept me angry, and anger is easier to bear."

Amy nodded. She examined every detail of the photo for a long time. When she looked up, the beginning of a smile played around her eyes. "You could at least have chosen someone with a less protruding nose."

She put aside the photograph and began to tear up her father's letter and all the letters she had written to him. Valerie watched her, uncomprehending at first, but when Amy handed her one, she smiled through her tears and ripped it up. Together, they filled the box with the shreds of Amy's longing and then took it out to the recycling bin. As the lid closed with a thud, they hugged until a passer-by stopped and stared at the two women embracing in a dark alleyway in the rain. Amy stuck her tongue out at him, and he hurried off in disgust. Amy took her mother's arm.

"Let's go back upstairs and open that bottle you brought. I think we both need a drink."

Chapter 25

Around lunchtime the next day, McCord was told by reception that a parcel had been handed in for him. As he picked it up, he recognized Amy's handwriting.

Hurriedly, he carried the parcel up to his office and was relieved to find that Calderwood had gone off somewhere. No need for anybody else to see what gifts he received from the woman everybody suspected him to be having an affair with.

On tearing open the paper, he discovered that Amy had given him a new tie – along with a card which merely said, 'I trust you will NOT come for dinner wearing a frayed tie.' Did the whole world know about his encounter with the shredder? Absent-mindedly, he stroked the wonderfully smooth light blue silk that had delicate white birds woven into it. They were meant to be swallows, he surmised, but the tails were all wrong. It was always the same; artists decorated everything with birds nowadays, cheerfully ignoring biological facts and claiming artistic licence.

Just then the phone rang. It was Amy.

"Did you get my present?" she asked.

"A moment ago," McCord said. "How did you know about the tie?" Then he remembered. "Did John tell you?"

"Of course not. He is far too much of a gentleman to comment on other people's wardrobe malfunctions. Martin, however, is different. Your efforts to hide the tie were in vain. It slipped out while you were talking to them. But he was still too polite to ask what had happened to the poor tie. So what was it?"

"I'll tell you another time. One more mention of ties, and I'm going to scream. The card mentioned a dinner. Have I missed something?"

"Mum and John would like you and Duncan to come to dinner on Friday," she said.

"Why?" he burst out. As he said the word, McCord realised how rude it sounded. "That is very nice," he added quickly. "What's the occasion?"

"To thank you both. They seem to think that you rescued me from the claws of a maniac who was about to rape and murder me."

"Which is what we actually did," McCord said.

Amy laughed. "Seven o'clock at John's flat in George Street, above the magazine. And no excuses."

At the sound of steps in the corridor and fearing it was the superintendent, McCord hastily stuffed the tie into his jacket pocket.

"Have to go, speak later."

He hung up.

Calderwood appeared in the door, eyeing his boss curiously.

"Everything okay?" he asked.

"Of course," McCord replied. "Did you get a dinner invitation from John and Amy's mother as well?"

"Yes, and not only that. See what Amy left for me at reception." With a big grin, Calderwood held up a brightly coloured tie. "Snazzy, isn't it?"

McCord felt a pang of jealousy. "It certainly makes a statement."

Suddenly, Calderwood looked troubled. "Is there anything wrong with the ties I'm wearing? Are they too boring?"

"Why don't you ask your butler?" McCord grumbled and turned his attention back to the case.

McGillivray's USB stick had been left on his desk, mocking him. Angrily, he stuck it into the port on his computer and opened the folder called 'Recovered Files'. DC Sutton had been right. There was nothing else on Lomax he could see; there were files several months old about stories McGillivray had been investigating but which clearly had come to nothing. But there was one other, more recent folder called 'CO'. When he opened it, McCord found a Word document detailing the CV of Charles Omerton from birth to the present. McGillivray had added notes about her visit to Mr Billington, Charles' old headmaster, but there was nothing beyond what Amy had already told him. Then there was a single photo file. McCord clicked on it.

"I'll be damned," he muttered. "Calderwood!" he called out. "Come here and look at this."

* * *

"Would you like to comment on this, sir?"

McCord had tracked down Charles Omerton in his constituency office and was not wasting time on polite chitchat. Calderwood sat next to his boss, his notebook at the ready.

"Ah." Omerton sighed when he saw the printed-out photograph. "How did you get hold of that?"

"Never mind," McCord said curtly. "What were you discussing with a prominent member of the Scottish Defence League and his delightful disciples? Your next manifesto?"

He pointed at the photo showing Omerton smiling and chatting to a man dressed in a black T-shirt and army trousers, surrounded by several youths with shaved heads and covered in SS, eagle and skull tattoos.

Omerton straightened his back.

"I was visiting a local youth club where parents had raised concerns about an infiltration of far-right activists who were recruiting in the area. By sheer coincidence, one of the SDL guys was there, and we started a discussion."

"And what exactly were you discussing? Whether the Holocaust actually happened or not?"

Calderwood's mouth twitched.

"I share your distaste of far-right ideology, DI McCord," Omerton said, making a show of being patient. "But as a politician, I often have to deal with people of a different persuasion. I was trying to understand what attracted young people to that organisation and how I might bring them back into the fold."

McCord tried a different tack.

"Who took the photo?"

"Martha McGillivray," Omerton said eventually. "I didn't know that she was following me around."

"You must have been annoyed by the picture," McCord said. "It wouldn't do your career any good if it was published."

"It certainly would not help," Omerton admitted.

"When did you realise the picture had been taken?"

"A week ago, when Martha McGillivray asked me for an interview and showed it to me. She seemed to think there was a neo-Nazi plot to seize power in Scotland, and that I was at the centre of it."

McCord did not join in with the MSP's laughter.

"And are you?"

Omerton's smile evaporated.

"Of course not. These are small groups of deluded individuals with a very warped sense of reality who might dream of the Fourth Reich. Thankfully our democratic institutions are strong enough to withstand a few demonstrations and unpleasant social media posts. I hope you are writing all this down, too, DC Calderwood."

"Every word," Calderwood said.

"These groups would be very keen to have the endorsement of an up-and-coming Conservative like yourself, though, wouldn't they?" asked McCord. "It would give them more credibility."

"I have never endorsed any racist or antisemitic views," Omerton said sharply. "This photo creates completely the wrong impression, and that is why I'm not keen to have it splashed all over the newspapers."

"And did Martha McGillivray threaten to do that?" McCord asked.

"She was not naïve," Omerton replied. "She knew I would sue her for libel if she claimed I had far-right sympathies. She was trying to find further 'evidence'; she even door-stepped my poor mother."

"It was very convenient for you that she died, and that her laptop also disappeared, wasn't it?"

"Careful now," Omerton said quietly, all affability gone. "You seem to go from accusing me of being a neo-Nazi to being a murderer. Surely, you are aware that you need evidence for such serious allegations. But there can't be any evidence because I am neither. This conversation is now over."

He rose from his chair and held the door open.

"Did you ask Kirsty Hall to delete the picture from Martha's backup file, or was that her idea?" McCord asked on his way out.

"I have nothing further to say," Omerton replied and shut the door firmly behind them.

* * *

"What did you make of that?" McCord asked Calderwood when they were back out on the street.

"He was clearly rattled," Calderwood said. "But it could have been an unlucky coincidence that he and the SDL guy were there at the same time."

McCord was sceptical.

"Even so. This photograph in the wrong hands could put an end to all his hopes of high office."

"And he met McGillivray within the time frame of her being poisoned," Calderwood said. "But then, it sounds as if her visit came as a surprise to him, so he would not have had time to get the poison ready."

"No, but his girlfriend had," McCord pointed out. "McGillivray's death gave Kirsty everything: a career-saver for her boyfriend, a big scoop and an inheritance for herself. That's another reason why we need to bring her in again. But first, we need to dig deeper around Lomax and the Bronze Age settlement. Get PC Dharwan to go through all the files again."

* * *

Back at St Leonard's, McCord was waylaid by Superintendent Gilchrist.

"Any progress on the McGillivray case?" he asked.

"Yes, sir," McCord replied.

He had to think quickly. Gilchrist would not like to hear that he had been less than deferential to a Conservative MSP with a so far unblemished reputation or that he was about to interrogate a journalist, so he decided on a minimalist version.

"A former friend of the victim had motive, means and opportunity. We have also uncovered possible corruption in the awarding of the contract for the West Middleton project, which gives the owner of Lomax Construction a strong motive for murder. We're following up both leads."

"Excellent. Carry on the good work and keep me posted."

Having given his troops the necessary encouragement, Gilchrist withdrew into his office.

Chapter 26

Sitting in Interview Room 2, Drummond Wilson, a short, tubby man in his forties, was the personification of a guilty conscience.

"I swear I never falsified an EIA in my life! I've been working at this company for ten years, and there has never been any suggestion–"

"Be careful what you swear to," McCord interrupted him. "You might well have to swear in court, and perjury carries a two-year prison sentence."

Wilson's complexion went from vivid red to deathly pale. "You can ask my boss–"

"We have, and she confirms that there have never been any complaints about you," McCord said. "But the question is how closely anybody read your reports in the past. Unfortunately, this time somebody dug a little bit deeper, excuse the pun, and after a brief excursion, found evidence of a Bronze Age settlement that you seem either to have missed or to have deliberately left out of the findings in the report."

"If there is a Bronze Age settlement on the site, it was a genuine mistake!" Wilson wailed.

"Now wait a minute," McCord said in his frighteningly quiet voice. "Taking a backhander is one thing, murder is quite another. Withholding evidence in a homicide investigation is a serious matter."

"I have nothing to do with any murder!" Wilson's voice had taken on a hysterical undertone.

"Maybe you were not even aware that you were part of it, so if you help us to understand what you did or didn't do, then *we* can help *you*," Calderwood said, playing his good cop role.

Wilson straightened up as if to steel himself against any further questions. "I conducted the assessment in good faith, and if I made a mistake, I sincerely apologise."

McCord leaned forward.

"If you took a bribe, we will find a paper trail, sooner or later. And the judge won't like the fact that you've been lying to the police during the investigation."

"The judge won't like that at all," Calderwood echoed.

"So, I'm asking you for the last time," McCord said, "how much did Godfrey Lomax pay you to turn a blind eye to the Bronze Age settlement?"

There was the briefest flicker of Wilson's eyelids before he answered.

"Godfrey Lomax never paid me any bribes, and I'll swear to that fact in court."

McCord took a deep breath and stood up.

"If you want to play it that way," he said, "fine. But we have the necessary evidence to show that your report was misleading, so we will be having another conversation with you. Don't leave the country without informing us. Interview concluded at 15.32. DC Calderwood is going to see you out."

Alone in the interview room, McCord rested his head on his folded hands. Several times now, he had seemed so tantalizingly close to a solution, yet every time the last piece of the puzzle eluded him. The longer the investigation continued, the harder it would be to find evidence, and he could not afford another failure like last time.

When he lifted his head again, he saw that the screen on his phone had lit up. After the interview he had forgotten to switch off the mute function. He jumped up, suddenly energised again. DC Sutton had something for him. Returning the call, he pressed the phone to his ear to be sure he caught every sparse word she would utter.

"What have you got, DC Sutton?"

"No calls by Lomax after your meeting."

"No calls?" McCord could not believe it.

"First call, an hour later, to his mother," DC Sutton said.

McCord sat down again, deflated. He had been so sure.

"Thank you. Please check previous records, particularly for calls to a Drummond Wilson. And keep checking his phone records every few hours in case he makes that call later."

The line went dead.

No call? It could mean only one of two things: either Lomax was innocent, or he was very cunning indeed.

McCord should have gone back to his office but suddenly he felt drained of all energy. His mind drifted to southern wetlands where thin-legged waders gracefully stalked across the mud, probing it with their long beaks for the delicacies buried within; then his inner eye rose to follow the elegant flight of the majestic eagle in the open sky.

An urgent knock on the door brought him crashing back to reality.

"Come in," he called out wearily.

The door burst open.

"There you are, sir," PC Dharwan panted, "I've been looking everywhere for you. I know who Gill is."

* * *

"Let's hear it then," McCord said when he, PC Dharwan and Calderwood were all assembled in his office.

PC Dharwan spread out a map of the area covering the proposed town of West Middleton. She circled it with red pen. In the south-eastern corner, covering roughly a quarter of the future West Middleton, she made another circle.

"This area here is called Brookfield, currently a working farm. Lomax Construction has offered the owner a cool million for his land."

Calderwood whistled through his teeth.

"And here" – she placed a cross within the small circle near to where the main access road was marked – "Martha McGillivray and Matt Branston found the Bronze Age brooch and potshard."

"And the name of the farmer is…" began McCord, who by now knew what had happened.

"Gillespie," PC Dharwan announced proudly. "McGillivray had no time to finish the message. Hamish Gillespie stood to lose the chance of a very comfortable early retirement if the settlement was discovered."

McCord nodded, pulled out his phone and started typing a message.

When he had finished, he raised his head and smiled.

"Great job, PC Dharwan. I've messaged DC Sutton to see if there are any communications between Gillespie, Lomax and Drummond Wilson. DC Calderwood and I are going to Brookfield now to ask Farmer Gillespie a few difficult questions. And you are coming with us."

PC Dharwan folded the map, beaming with pleasure.

"Yes, sir. Ready when you are."

* * *

"What the hell is going on here?" McCord shouted as they approached the field on Brookfield Farm to which PC Dharwan had guided them. The narrow country road was cordoned off with tape, and a sign had been erected urging caution during 'construction work'.

The field where Martha McGillivray and Matt Branston had found the Bronze Age artefacts had been used as pasture for centuries. Now it resembled a quarry. A gaping hole in the ground, at least fifty yards long and almost as wide, had been made by a huge digger that scooped the soil into the trailer of a waiting lorry. Over the deafening noise, the digger driver could not hear McCord's shouting, so the detectives ran towards the giant machine waving their arms. Eventually, the driver noticed them and switched off the engine. The sudden silence was a relief, and McCord could finally hear himself think again. With surprising agility, the driver dismounted his vehicle and strode towards the detectives.

"What the hell were you thinking, coming so close to an operating digger? You could have been killed!" He pointed to the sign. "Can't you read?"

McCord whipped out his ID.

"Contrary to malicious rumours circulating in the press, we are not quite illiterate. We were trying to prevent you from destroying a valuable archaeological site. Are you Hamish Gillespie?"

The man looked at McCord as if he were mad.

"Of course not. No one, not even farmers can work a machine like this baby. You need training for that. What archaeological site are you talking about anyway? I'm preparing the ground for new cattle sheds."

"New cattle sheds? A couple of months before all this is going to be ploughed under to build a new town? Aye right," McCord said, his voice dripping with sarcasm.

The driver shrugged.

"Nothing to do with me. The farmer is paying me to clear the ground. What he's doing with it afterwards is his business."

"Not if it is illegal," McCord pointed out. "Then it becomes our business. Stop your work here immediately. Where is Farmer Gillespie?"

The driver shrugged again.

"Probably in the farmhouse. Back along this road, and at the next junction turn right."

McCord waved to the lorry driver who had watched them from a safe distance to come over.

While PC Dharwan was taking the details and statements of the two men, McCord phoned the station and instructed PC Turner to organise some archaeologists to come out here to assess the damage. And shortly afterwards, PC Dharwan had the great satisfaction of arresting Farmer Gillespie.

Chapter 27

When Amy parked her mother's ancient MG at the Kingdom Country Club in Fife, Martin whistled through his teeth.

"Nice venue for an award ceremony; this event must have set Omerton back a bob or two."

Amy shrugged. "He's a member of the golf club, so I suppose he'll get a rebate."

As they entered the gleaming and ostentatious foyer, Amy remembered her first case, which had brought her to this country club, and smiled at the memory. To her relief, Stephanie, the receptionist with whom she'd had dealings before, was not on duty; it was a young man who pointed them in the direction of the McIntosh Suite where the Kingdom of Fife Young Conservative Award ceremony would be held.

It was a large, brightly lit room with floor-to-ceiling windows that would have given a splendid view onto the North Sea. By now, it was completely dark outside, and the blinds, depicting a sun-drenched seashore, had been drawn. Amy shook her head at the garish colours and surveyed the room instead.

Small groups of smartly dressed people were milling about, mainly parents with teenagers, some of whom looked ill at ease in these plush surroundings. A couple of waiters moved about discreetly with trays of drinks and canapés, and a short, thin man in jeans and sweatshirt was setting up a podium and microphone on a makeshift stage at the other end of the room.

"There you are!"

Kirsty Hall made a beeline for Amy and was duly introduced to Martin.

"Good to see you both. I do hope it goes well," she added quietly after they had settled at one of the small tables dotted around the room. "Charles has been quite nervous; this is the first time he's run such an event. Oh," – she jumped up and nodded in the direction of an elegant woman who was approaching them – "here is his mum. You must meet her."

"Sandra, this is Amy Thornton and Martin Eden from *Forth Write* magazine," Hall introduced them. "Sandra Omerton."

"I'm so glad you could come!" Sandra Omerton welcomed Amy and Martin, but not before she had given Hall a hug. "Charles will be thrilled to see you both. He told me that you are writing a feature about him for your magazine. And this is such a worthwhile cause to attend. It was all Charles' idea, you know."

"I'm not sure how this works, exactly," Martin said. "How are the shortlisted candidates chosen?"

Sandra Omerton smiled and pointed behind them.

"I don't know all the ins and outs of it, but you can ask the man himself!"

They turned to watch Charles Omerton make his way towards them, greeting people and shaking hands as he moved confidently across the floor. When he had finally reached Amy's table, he seemed to have eyes only for his girlfriend. He grasped her hands, pulled her towards him and whispered something in her ear. Hall blushed and shook her head, looking indignant and pleased at the same time. Then Charles Omerton caught his mother's eye and remembered his manners. He turned to Amy and Martin with a beaming smile.

"The esteemed members of the press – welcome! It is great to see you at a gathering that shows me in a rather better light–"

"Mr Eden was asking about the Young Conservative Award and how it works; you can explain it much better than I can," his mother interrupted him.

"Now don't hide your light under a bushel, Mum, after all, it was your idea."

Sandra Omerton shook her head.

"Nonsense, you put it all together."

"If you insist. Well" – he turned to Martin – "the idea is to encourage young people to live according to modern Conservative values – the way I understand them. Caring for people, protecting the environment, making innovations in business and science, being creative. Headmasters in all the schools in Fife were sent a form where they could nominate one of their pupils for any of the categories. They had to explain why these young people deserve the award and submit some evidence."

"But surely, these children are not paying members of the Conservative and Unionist Party?" Martin objected.

"You are right, of course," Charles Omerton said, "but I hope that one day they will be. Headmasters rarely pass up the chance of their pupils winning an award and getting into the papers. It is an award *from* the Conservative Party, rather than an award for *being* a member of the Conservatives. One of our winners tonight, the boy over there, is called Brodie Simpson. He is well on course to be the local candidate for the Greens once he is eighteen. He designed a recycling scheme for his school that resulted in a reduction in unrecyclable waste by 80%. Tonnes of waste avoided because of *one* person making an effort. And I want to show that if I get my way, these are the kind of people who will have a home in the Conservative Party."

Amy nodded appreciatively but Martin was slightly more cynical.

"What about Westminster?" he asked. "You seem to be in a bit of a minority, aren't you? Are you sure that you are in the right party?"

Omerton laughed.

"Change has to start somewhere. Now, if you'll excuse me, I need to get ready for my address. Enjoy the evening."

With a slight wave, he disappeared into the adjoining room. Sandra Omerton also excused herself; she had to mix with the other guests.

"He *is* gorgeous," Amy said to Hall with a wink, "and he seems to be very much in love with you."

Hall blushed again.

"Yes, I believe I have actually won the jackpot with Charles."

"What did he mean when he said, 'showing him in a better light' – better light than what?" Amy asked.

Hall gave her a strange look.

"That photograph, of course, that your detective gave him so much grief about. Maybe *you* can convince DI McCord that Charles is not a reincarnation of Hitler."

Amy nodded hastily.

"Of course, the *photograph*. I've told DI McCord already, but he never listens to me," she said in mock exasperation. "Excuse me a minute."

Amy picked up her handbag and rushed towards the door. In case Hall was watching, she walked quickly towards the ladies', but then turned towards the exit and found a quiet spot behind a brutally trimmed boxwood plant about ten yards from the entrance.

"McCord," she snapped when he had picked up the call, "what incriminating photograph do you have of Charles Omerton?"

"A photo of him meeting one of the leaders of the Scottish Defence League," he told her.

Amy gasped.

"What?! Saint Charles in cahoots with the neo-Nazis? And it didn't occur to you to tell me that? I'm at an event run by him, and I seem to be the only one who hasn't got a clue what is going on!"

"I'm sorry I didn't give you a step-by-step account of my day," McCord said defensively. "We have been kind of busy saving the country's heritage and arresting people."

"Still, it would be helpful to know whom I'm dealing with. You said yourself, I should be careful."

"You're not planning to take him home with you, are you?" McCord asked. "You know he is spoken for by a woman who might be prepared to go to great lengths to protect him from predators like you."

"Ha, bloody ha. You don't get it, do you. Hall is here, too. She is only interested in me because she thinks that I am close to the investigation. I felt like a right numpty in there just now, and I don't know if I managed to cover up my complete lack of inside information. You've let me down."

"I'm sorry," McCord said again, more convincingly this time. "What event is this anyway?"

"An award ceremony for young people who do great things. One of Charles' ideas. I thought it would be a good opportunity to observe him and Hall together."

"Might well be. But be careful. Given your recent record of damage to people and property, I should not be at all surprised if–"

"Och, shut up, McCord," Amy growled, but she couldn't help laughing. "And anyway, Martin is with me."

"Excellent." McCord sounded relieved. "What impression have you got of Omerton and Hall?"

"They seem very much in love. He is very demonstrative and flirted with her right in front of everybody. And she – how did she phrase it? – 'hit the jackpot', that was it."

"Hm, strange way to talk about your boyfriend," McCord said. "I think that Hall is quite calculating. Anyway, don't ask any questions that might make them suspicious. Just smile and keep your eyes open."

"Thanks for the lecture. By the way, which poor citizen have you arrested today?"

"I shouldn't tell you, of course, but it is Hamish Gillespie, who owns part of the land West Middleton is going to be built on. He stood to lose a million pounds if the fact that there is a Bronze Age settlement on his land had been made public. He has tried to destroy the whole site in the past couple of days."

"Wow, that is certainly a big, fat motive. Do you think he could have killed McGillivray?"

"Not one hundred per cent sure. Another thirty hours of alibi to check." McCord sighed. "By the way, I haven't thanked you properly for your gift. I promise to wear the tie to dinner on Friday as directed. And for future reference, a swallow's tail is not three times as long as its body. The poor bird would tie itself into a knot trying to fly like that."

Amy snorted. "I'll be sure to tell the award-winning designer she got it wrong. Has Calderwood said anything about his tie?"

"He thinks it is 'snazzy'. How come he gets a snazzy tie, and I get one embroidered with deformed birds?"

Amy laughed.

"Your lack of gratitude is appalling, as always. Well, I'd better let you get on with your investigation. Sounds as if you might have managed to catch McGillivray's killer at long last. Oh, and of course, this conversation never happened. Your phone will explode in five seconds."

With a giggle, she hung up.

Only now did she notice the almost imperceptible film of moisture that clung to her. Only in Scotland can one get wet without rain falling; microscopic waterdrops seem to float in the air, caressing the skin and almost apologetically soaking one's clothes; the gentlest reproach for being careless enough to go outside without a waterproof.

Shivering, Amy rushed inside and dried her face, hands and hair with one of the luxuriously thick, scented hand towels in the toilets. When she arrived back at the suite, Hall and Martin were engaged in a lively discussion about the elusive economic revival of the former mining villages in Fife. Both turned to her, and Amy noticed Hall's eyes hanging on her glistening outfit.

"Gone for a walk?" Hall asked casually.

"I wasn't feeling well all of a sudden," Amy said. "But I'm fine now. I just needed a breath of fresh air."

Martin scanned her face with a worried frown.

"Are you sure you're okay?"

"Yes, absolutely," Amy said brightly. "Look! The show is about to start."

They turned to the stage where a spotlight was turned on Charles Omerton, enveloping him in a magical golden glow.

Chapter 28

Hamish Gillespie of Brookfield Farm was a ruddy-faced fifty-four-year-old with a bull's neck and a donkey's bloody-mindedness. His protruding belly and trunk-like thighs forced him to move his chair a considerable distance back from the table, so that he had difficulty reaching the cup of tea which Calderwood had ungraciously placed in front of him. After one sip, however, Gillespie desisted from any further exertion as, judging by his face, it was not worth the effort. His legs were planted wide apart, and he kept his thick arms folded across his chest, making it quite clear that he was not in a mood to be bossed about or intimidated.

Unfortunately for him, McCord, after traipsing through a muddy field and soiling his dry-clean-only suit, was not concerned about peace and harmony either. He had moved right up to the table, sitting very upright to seem as tall as possible. Calderwood was watching with interest as the two alpha males prepared themselves for battle.

"Mr Gillespie, you have been arrested on suspicion of wilful damage to a site of historical interest, bribery and conspiracy to illegally obtain planning permission for the West Middleton project. What do you have to say to that?"

Hamish Gillespie looked as if there was plenty he would like to say but instead, he weighed his words carefully.

"I had no idea that there was a site of 'historical interest'," he said, exaggeratedly miming the quotation marks in the air, "on my farm. And on *my* farm, I can dig as much as I like."

"You stood to lose one million pounds if the Bronze Age settlement were to be discovered on your land," McCord said. "I put it to you that you bribed the surveyor, Drummond Wilson, to falsify his EIA of the area and to conceal the existence of the Bronze Age settlement on your land."

"You can put to me what you bloody well like," Gillespie retorted. "I haven't seen any evidence that this settlement exists. And even if it does, this fellow Wilson must be totally incompetent. That's not my problem. It was Mr Lomax that hired him."

McCord pointed at the file he had put on the desk, for show rather than any specific purpose.

"Interesting that you mention Mr Lomax. His interests and yours coincide beautifully. Both of you were in line to lose a lot of money because of this discovery." McCord leaned forward. "Did Mr Lomax pay you to sort this little problem out? Did he perhaps persuade Mr Wilson to bury the settlement in his report?"

Gillespie did not appear to appreciate the pun.

"I have no idea what Mr Lomax did or didn't do," he said. "I only know I didn't do anything. I'd have thought that the police have better things to do than chasing after bits of old pottery."

"How did you know that it was pottery that was found on your land?" McCord asked.

Gillespie lost his countenance, but only for a second.

"I didn't. But they always find pottery on such sites, don't they?"

McCord was getting fed up with the man. He stood up and walked around the table until he stood next to Gillespie. Then he bent down as if sharing a secret.

"Look here, Mr Gillespie, between ourselves, I don't give a damn about old pottery either. But I am conducting a *murder* inquiry, and the *murder* victim's last message before she died a painful death ended with *your* name."

He observed with great satisfaction that Gillespie's arms had dropped to his side, and he was now gripping his chair.

"In my experience," McCord continued, straightening up again, "before murder victims die, they send only two types of messages if they have the chance. The first type is a message to their loved ones. No offence, Mr Gillespie, but in Martha McGillivray's case I think we can safely rule out that possibility. The second type is almost always an attempt to tell the world who killed them. So, my colleague and I" – he pointed to Calderwood who was scrutinising Gillespie's face that was now oscillating between anger and fear – "can't help thinking that you and Mr Lomax – he was mentioned in her last message as well – had something to do with her death."

Propelled by sheer panic, Gillespie jumped up from his chair and turned on McCord.

"Hang on a minute! Murder? This is crazy!"

Like a flash, Calderwood moved between his boss and Gillespie, who retreated with his hands up in surrender.

"Sit down, Mr Gillespie," McCord commanded.

Seeing that the farmer obeyed and made no further move, Calderwood positioned himself by the door.

McCord spoke very quietly.

"We are going to check all your calls, emails and bank transactions. We are going to re-interview Mr Wilson, who by the way seems very concerned about the charges coming his way. And we'll talk to Mr Lomax. Again. It might take some time, but we will certainly find out exactly what was going on between the three of you. And then we will charge you, and most likely the other two, with fraud and possibly murder. DC Calderwood, accompany Mr Gillespie to his cell. Interview suspended at 18.23."

* * *

McCord rang the bell at his father's flat with some resentment. In the past, he would just walk in, using his own key, but now he felt he had to announce his arrival as if he were a visiting stranger. And what he might come across if he turned up unannounced, he did not even want to contemplate. He was somebody who was invited for dinner now, so that would be the end of their curry-and-chess nights. And what would that woman be like? What if his dad, in his desperation for a renewed love life, had fallen for some harpy? Was that why his dad had kept her a secret from him?

The door swinging open with a flourish put a stop to his dark musings. Keith McCord looked dapper in chinos and a crisp white shirt, and he had liberally applied aftershave. McCord still wore his work suit, its trouser legs encrusted with mud from Gillespie's farm, and he wished now he had shaved before he came.

"Come in, come in," Keith said, beaming. "Dinner is almost ready."

McCord followed him into the living room where a shapely woman was bent over the table, folding napkins. She straightened up, twisting a strand of dark brown hair streaked with grey behind her ear, and put her hand out with a shy smile. Clearly, she was as nervous about meeting McCord as he was about meeting her. He shook a warm hand and relaxed a little.

"I'm Clare. Very nice to meet you, Russell," she said. "Your dad has told me so much about you."

"What have you been telling Clare?" McCord asked his dad in mock suspicion.

"Only that you are awfully clever, know everything about birds and almost single-handedly keep the people of Edinburgh safe," Clare answered in Keith's place.

"Well, I'm not doing a very good job at the moment, am I?" McCord observed. "We still haven't charged anybody with the murder of Martha McGillivray."

"I'm sure you'll nail him in the end," Keith announced with conviction.

Clare winked at McCord. "I can't wait for *Forth Write* to come out on Saturday. I hope Amy Thornton is writing another series like she did after the McAdie and the Rock Killer cases. I'm told she's quite a girl."

"Don't you start as well," McCord blurted out.

He saw his dad wince at his rudeness and blushed in embarrassment, but Clare just laughed. "Fair enough, not a word more. I'll go and check the dinner."

She disappeared into the kitchen. Keith regarded his son triumphantly as if to say, 'I told you so!' He opened two bottles of beer and poured Clare a glass of white wine that sat in a new ice-filled cooler on the table. McCord felt quite emotional. He had never seen his father so happy.

Clare came back from the kitchen carrying a large dish containing crispy brown chicken, surrounded by glistening potatoes and crunchy vegetables. It smelt wonderful.

"After two curries this week, I thought you might like something different," she said with a little smile to McCord.

"It looks delicious," McCord said truthfully.

"And after dinner," she announced, "while you play your chess game, I am going to finish my book. It's the latest mystery by Linda Hagan; I can't wait to find out who the killer is."

McCord stuck his fork into the succulent chicken breast. Maybe having a stepmother wasn't so bad after all.

Chapter 29

A couple of days later, McCord left it to Calderwood's more sympathetic nature to take the statement of Professor Thurrock, the visibly upset expert from the Edinburgh Archaeological Field Society who had inspected Brookfield Farm with the help of some colleagues.

"It is, or rather would have been, an exceptional site," the professor said. "There is no doubt that there is a Bronze Age settlement there, but part of it has been completely destroyed by this act of senseless vandalism. I hope whoever did this will rot in jail for decades!"

"That will depend on the outcome of our inquiry," Calderwood said diplomatically, and received a nod of confirmation from McCord, "but he will certainly be charged. Is there enough left of the site to warrant a withdrawal of the planning permission?"

"Absolutely," the professor said, his eyes glistening from barely held back tears. "That's what makes it so maddening. It's quite a large settlement, and not the only one in the Borders. You probably know of Eildon Hill? No? Well worth a visit. It's near Melrose, not far away from the Gorebridge site. Another Bronze Age settlement, slightly older than this one, but both sites were probably home to the Selgovae tribe who lived on the banks of the Tweed–"

"That's all very interesting, I'm sure," Calderwood interrupted him, "but it's purely academic now that most of the part of the site that was on his land has been destroyed, is it not?"

"Vandalised would be a more appropriate word," said the professor. "However, as far as I can make out, it's not a complete disaster. You see, it's such a large site, the farmer never had a chance to destroy the whole settlement nor remove all the evidence of it, even on his land. I wonder why he even attempted to?"

"We'll ask him that very question. But he was about to lose one million pounds, and that tends to make people a tad irrational." When the professor opened his mouth, no doubt to express his disgust, Calderwood quickly continued. "In your opinion, knowing the extent of this Bronze Age settlement, should the West Middleton project be abandoned?"

The professor nodded vigorously.

"Work certainly should not start until the whole area has been mapped out and fully excavated. We can't simply bulldoze away four-thousand-year-old evidence of our history. My colleagues at the Archaeological Field Society and I are extremely grateful to you for saving this site for posterity."

"We were only doing our job," Calderwood said. "Thank you for coming in. We will let you know when the case comes to court."

After Calderwood had seen the professor out, he slumped into his chair.

"What do we do next?" he asked McCord.

"The correct question is: *who* next? Where would you go from here?"

"Drummond Wilson," Calderwood said without hesitation. "I reckon, he'll crack first."

McCord nodded appreciatively.

"Go and bring him in."

* * *

Drummond Wilson looked as if he had not had much sleep in the last few days. McCord, by contrast, was exceedingly cheerful.

"Now, Mr Wilson. Let's talk some more about the innocent mistake you made with the EIA for the West Middleton Project."

He paused until the surveyor began shifting in his seat. Then he continued in a voice normally used to inquire about the other person's last holiday.

"Can you explain where the £10,000 in cash came from that you have been depositing into your bank account in smaller batches over the past two weeks?"

Wilson's lower lip began to tremble, and McCord knew it would not take long.

"Because it is funny, you see, that Hamish Gillespie, the farmer and owner of the land on which the Bronze Age settlement is situated, withdrew the same amount, again in several batches, a few hours before you deposited yours."

It was always gratifying to see a suspect crumble under investigation; a confession saved everybody a lot of time and money; but more importantly, it would make Superintendent Gilchrist happy. And here it came.

"I have never done anything like this before, I swear," Wilson croaked.

McCord could have reminded him that he had sworn to a lie before. But McCord believed him this time, so he let it pass.

"And tell me, how was Godfrey Lomax involved in all this?" McCord asked.

"I believe he only heard about it from you. Gillespie told me Lomax turned up at his farm, furious, and asked what all this was about. Gillespie told him not to worry, he could make everything go away."

"But he didn't, did he," McCord said. "Instead, he made everything a lot worse."

* * *

Neither Gillespie nor Wilson was able to present a watertight alibi for the two days leading up to Martha McGillivray's murder. McCord had passed on the Lomax-Weatherspoon connection to the Scottish Office who would determine whether to pursue the allegations of corruption any further. In order to arrest them for McGillivray's murder, however, he needed more evidence than a councillor using his position and influence to gain planning permission for his son-in-law.

As far as McCord was concerned, all four men were still in the frame. But for all their greed and corruption, he could not see any one of these men concocting a poison from castor oil seeds and slipping it into Martha McGillivray's food or drink. There was somebody else, however, who fitted the bill much better.

* * *

Kirsty Hall was not at all impressed when she was interrupted at work and marched into an interview room for another grilling from the two detectives.

"What on earth is it now?" she demanded. "I have an appointment in an hour, an interview with the Moderator of the General Assembly of the Church of Scotland. He is not someone who is prepared to hang around waiting."

"Surely, for somebody who believes in eternal life, an hour or two is a minor matter," McCord said and closed the door behind them.

As they sat down, Hall leant forward belligerently and looked him straight in the eye, but McCord noticed that under the table, she wiped her palms on her thighs.

"We've had a more thorough examination of Martha's USB stick," McCord began. "Can you think what we might have found in the deleted files?"

Hall sat up defiantly.

"I suppose you are referring to the photograph Martha McGillivray took. Charles told me about your aggressive questioning."

"You are supposing correctly," McCord said. "The photograph of your boyfriend in a cosy chat with one of the most unpleasant characters in the neo-Nazi scene."

"Charles isn't a neo-Nazi," Hall said, "and people have no right to make assumptions on the basis of a snapshot."

McCord pretended to ponder this.

"You were not quite so scrupulous where Godfrey Lomax and Councillor Weatherspoon were concerned, were you? You were quite happy to suggest to your readership that they are corrupt and potentially even murderers?"

"I leave it up to the readers to make up their mind," she replied. "I genuinely believe that the West Middleton project stinks, and I *know* that Charles has nothing to do with fascists."

"And that makes it okay to conceal evidence from a police investigation?"

McCord waved away Hall's attempt to answer.

"It was a rhetorical question. I put it to you, Miss Hall, that you poisoned Martha McGillivray on 14th November at the SKYbar in Edinburgh by giving her champagne laced with ricin in order to prevent her from exposing your boyfriend as a neo-Nazi sympathiser, retain your inheritance and gain possession of Martha's files on the West Middleton project. You broke into your dead friend's flat, stole her backup files, deleted evidence and diverted our attention away from Lomax Construction until you had the opportunity to land the biggest scoop of your career. By pointing the finger at other suspects, like Shug McCain and Cameron Coates, you deflected any suspicion away from yourself. But no longer. If you confess and express remorse, the judge might consider the fact that you tried to protect the father of your unborn child and be more lenient in his sentencing."

"You are crazy," Hall whispered, her face white under the carefully applied makeup. "I didn't kill Martha; I was fond of her even if we had grown apart recently. I admit to taking the USB stick, but Martha had told me to get it in the event of her death. I did not kill her! You can't possibly have any proof. It is all conjecture and circumstantial evidence."

"I'm confident we'll find proof. Nowadays it is very difficult to hide any aspect of your life, and as we speak, officers are all over your flat, your car, your communications, bank accounts, everything. You'd really be better off coming clean now."

"No way," Hall said. "I can't admit to something I haven't done. Are you arresting me?"

"Not yet," McCord said, "but I was hoping you would see sense."

"Well, you were hoping wrong," she said. "Can I go back to work now?"

"For now," McCord said, "but don't leave the city without telling us."

Hall gave a snort of contempt.

"Well, I'll be taking the train from Waverley to Leuchars tonight at seven thirty. Charles' mum and I are going to watch him giving a speech in St Andrews – if that is acceptable to you?"

Her voice was dripping with sarcasm.

"I suppose so, but don't even think of going further afield without notifying us," McCord said.

"And first thing tomorrow, I shall contact my solicitor."

She got up and left with her head held high.

"Well, it was worth a try," Calderwood said. "But I do worry about finding conclusive evidence. She won't be daft enough to have a chemistry set sitting around her flat, will she, and anything else could be explained away by a clever defence lawyer."

McCord nodded.

"You've got a point, but that's not something I want to hear right now."

Chapter 30

"We are delighted that you were both able to come," John Campbell said as he shook McCord's and Calderwood's hands warmly when they arrived at his spacious George Street flat.

"Thank you for the invitation," Calderwood said, handing a large bouquet of flowers to Valerie.

A delicious smell emanated from the kitchen. McCord saw the beautifully laid table and the effort his kind hosts had made and berated himself for being unable to relax into what should be a most enjoyable evening. Something undefinable was buzzing around inside his brain, trying to reveal itself, and he could not shake off the feeling that he should be back at the office, more carefully going through the McGillivray file. And why was the voice of Zane Smith sounding in his ears, as if trying to tell him something?

"...and, of course, the one who is *not* here is our Amy," Valerie was saying, censure in her voice. "But she's texted me. She'll be here in a minute."

"I shall fetch the champagne then," John said and disappeared into the kitchen.

"I'm afraid, I'm driving," McCord called after him. "Can I have a soft drink, please?"

"No, you can't," Valerie said, pulling his arm into hers. "After all, you saved our Amy, yet *again*, and you must be allowed to take some time off the job. You are most welcome to sleep in our spare room."

Valerie smiled innocently, while Calderwood had a face like thunder. McCord said nothing, wondering if Amy would stay over as well. He had some difficulty suppressing the whole maelstrom of conflicting emotions which engulfed him.

Valerie broke the embarrassed silence.

"I don't know how you manage that commute to Portobello every day. Don't you hate it?"

"Every single day," McCord replied. "But the birdwatching round there is amazing."

"Not tonight, though," Valerie said. "A night like this is for being cosy indoors with good friends."

John came through with a tray of glasses and a bottle of Moët & Chandon. He expertly opened it and started pouring the liquid bubbles into glasses. As he handed one to McCord, they heard the door open, and Amy breezed into the room, flinging her bag and coat onto the sofa and bringing in with her the cold, fresh air of a clear winter evening. "Hello, everybody, great to see you all!"

Then her eye fell on the glass in McCord's hand. "Ah, just what the doctor ordered."

With a cheeky laugh, she took the drink from him, lifted the glass in a mock toast and took a big swig. "Nice tie, by the way!" She giggled.

"Amy!" Valerie scolded her. "Where are your manners! That was DI McCord's glass!"

"You shouldn't be drinking anyway, you're driving," Amy said to McCord, "unless you're staying the night at my flat, of course."

McCord froze.

John and Valerie looked aghast.

"I must apologise for my daughter's behaviour," Valerie said, giving Amy the death stare. "One should always blame the mother."

McCord had not been listening. His brain had gone into overdrive, cerebral wires making connections. In his mind, he was reading Zane Smith's statement again and going over his interview with Kirsty Hall earlier.

"Oh my God," he whispered. He pulled out his phone to see what time it was. "Oh my God," he said again, "fifteen minutes. We only have fifteen minutes! Come on, Calderwood, we've got to go!"

"What?!" Calderwood's gloomy expression was replaced by surprise.

"We've got fifteen minutes!" McCord shouted. "Come on!"

"To do what?" Amy asked, but she was already putting on her coat.

Stunned, John and Valerie stood there, as all their guests rushed out of the door.

* * *

McCord, Calderwood and Amy were running along George Street until they reached the Juke that was parked fifty yards away. McCord slapped the blue flashing light on the roof and set off before Calderwood had even managed to shut his door. Thankfully, the worst of the rush hour was over, but the Friday night traffic was still heavy. Cars moved hastily out of their way as McCord tore down Hanover Street and turned into Princes Street where a tram and a bus blocked their way. McCord swore and honked his horn until the tram moved and he was able to overtake the bus.

McCord made no attempt to explain this mad rush, and seeing that they were doing sixty miles an hour through the city centre, both Calderwood and Amy were glad to see McCord concentrate on the road. With screeching tyres, he took the corner into Waverley Bridge and turned left into the railway station where access was categorically forbidden to cars. He drove down until he came to a barrier, slammed on the brakes and jumped out of the car.

"Come on!" he shouted to his companions, quite unnecessarily, as they were already right behind him, wondering what on earth was going on.

Running towards the platforms, McCord scanned the noticeboard for the train to Leuchars. Platform 15. The digital clock underneath proclaimed it was 19.28. McCord squeezed past the queuing passengers who were starting to complain. With Calderwood and Amy hot on his heels, he held his ID under the nose of the ScotRail employee guarding the access to the platforms.

"Police, let us through. Has the Leuchars train come in yet?"

"There it is coming in now," the employee said proudly, "dead on time."

They saw the lights approaching the station and sprinted towards the platform. Calderwood, being the fittest of the three, had overtaken McCord but not knowing what they were actually trying to do, he turned round.

"Get her away from the train," McCord gasped.

They had reached Platform 15. Quite a distance along, they saw Kirsty Hall and Sandra Omerton standing on the edge of the platform, examining something on the track. The train had come through the small tunnel and was now entering the station, its headlights two giant eyes. Sandra Omerton suddenly moved behind Hall and put her hands on her shoulder blades.

"Watch out!" Calderwood screamed at the top of his voice just before it was drowned out by the high-pitched screeching of the train's brakes as it slowed towards the buffers.

Hall turned and saw the detectives and Amy running towards her, waving and shouting, at the very moment Sandra Omerton pushed her backwards towards the track. Stunned by the sudden attack and the hatred shooting out of Sandra Omerton's eyes, Hall stepped back until her heels hung over the edge of the platform. The deafening sound of the train's horn jolted her back into fighting mode, and she struggled with her attacker in a deadly embrace, swirling round along the platform's edge.

Calderwood leapt forward and managed to grab Hall's arm.

McCord and Amy were only yards away, and in that one second, they both saw the defiance and then the realisation of defeat in Sandra Omerton's eyes. She let go of Hall, turned towards the relentlessly approaching train and let herself fall in front of it as it slowly thundered past.

In the cacophony of screeching brakes, the incessant howling of the horn and the screams of the people on the platform, Calderwood yanked Hall away from the edge and held her down until the train had finally come to a halt. Then everything went deadly quiet.

Chapter 31

It took a good while to clear the platform and take witness statements. Kirsty Hall and the train driver had been taken away by ambulance to be treated for shock, but not before the paramedics had severely reprimanded McCord for blocking the way of the emergency vehicles with his illegally abandoned car.

McCord studiously avoided looking at the scene on the track that was being examined by the forensics team, while the stationmaster moaned yet again about the disruption of a train service and the necessity to organise a bus replacement for disgruntled passengers who would be clamouring for a refund. Now, overworked ScotRail staff had to reschedule their rotas as the train driver would probably be unfit for service for weeks, if he could ever erase from his memory the vision of the body falling in front of him.

McCord just nodded. He did not say that this was yet another violent death that would also stay with him forever, and that he would store it away with all the other horrors he had witnessed in his job.

* * *

Back at St Leonard's, Amy organised coffee and snacks to sustain McCord as he oversaw the complex process of clearing up after a human tragedy. Afterwards, she sat uncharacteristically quiet on her chair behind the door, reading something on her phone.

McCord watched her delicate fingers scrolling down page after page. Amy must have sensed something because she looked up, smiling.

"I'm checking social media. Everybody is talking about what happened tonight, and not all of it is complimentary to Police Scotland."

"It never is." McCord sighed and went back to his report.

At ten thirty, McCord had finished and leant back in his chair, exhausted.

Calderwood then came back from the hospital to report that Kirsty Hall and the train driver had recovered sufficiently to give their statements. Charles Omerton had turned up, distraught on finding out that his mother had tried to kill his partner and unborn child and then committed suicide.

"Imagine having to deal with that," Calderwood said. "But from the way they were holding on to each other, I think they're going to get through this."

"What made you realise that it was Sandra Omerton?" Amy asked McCord, unable to contain her curiosity any longer.

"The champagne," McCord said. "When you took my glass from me, it was exactly like the scene in the SKYbar that Zane Smith had described. Hall had not *given* McGillivray the champagne, McGillivray had taken it *off her*. The poison was never meant for McGillivray at all but for Hall, although it was an incredible stroke of luck for Sandra Omerton that McGillivray happened to take the drink."

Amy was still confused.

"But why would Sandra Omerton want to kill Hall – and her own grandchild? And why was it a stroke of luck that McGillivray was killed by accident?"

"Hall explained everything to me at the hospital," Calderwood said. "She is still badly shaken up, but she is quite clear how everything happened. According to Hall, Sandra Omerton was never going to accept her."

"But Hall told me herself that Sandra Omerton had come round to the idea of her being with Charles, and she was very affectionate towards Hall when I saw them together," Amy said.

Calderwood shook his head. "That's what Hall thought at the time. But now she is sure that Sandra Omerton only put on a brave face when she realised that Charles was not going to break up with her. Sandra Omerton still considered Hall to be a hindrance to her precious son's political career. She had given her life to Charles' success, and she was not going to let anything, or anybody for that matter, interfere with her ambitions for her son."

"But didn't the prospect of a grandchild change her mind?" Amy asked.

Calderwood shook his head.

"Hall told me that Sandra Omerton, when she was told about the pregnancy, had expected her and Charles to marry asap, and she urged Hall to devote her life to support Charles in his career as she had spent her life doing. But Hall told her that she wanted to keep working as a journalist and saw no need to get married in a hurry."

"Sandra Omerton must have been horrified by the photograph of Charles and the neo-Nazis?" Amy asked.

"Absolutely," Calderwood said. "When McGillivray turned up on her doorstep with that photograph that could have ruined Charles' career, Sandra Omerton tried to get Hall to use her connection to McGillivray to get hold of the photo and destroy it. Maybe Sandra Omerton saw it as a kind of test of her loyalty to Charles. But Hall told her it was impossible to stop McGillivray, which Sandra Omerton must have regarded as a cop-out and an utter betrayal. When Hall did get hold of the photo later, she didn't tell Sandra Omerton that she had deleted the picture from the files."

Amy looked at Calderwood, aghast.

"So, Sandra Omerton decided that Hall was not sufficiently loyal to her son, saw all her plans for his political future being jeopardised and decided that Hall needed to be removed from his life by any means necessary?"

Calderwood nodded. "And when McGillivray turned up dead instead, it nicely solved the issue of the photograph for Sandra Omerton, but she had to have another go at killing Hall."

Amy shuddered at the thought that a mother's love could turn into such callousness.

"But what about McGillivray's message to Hall warning her of Lomax?" she asked McCord.

"That was what put us on the wrong track from the outset of this case," McCord replied. "I think McGillivray was preoccupied with Lomax and Gillespie and the corruption she suspected. I believe she had no idea who killed her or maybe didn't even realise that she *had* been poisoned. She probably just felt that she was dying and wanted to pass on her last investigation to Hall."

"But do we have sufficient proof against Sandra Omerton?" Calderwood asked his boss.

McCord shrugged.

"We all saw that she was trying to push Hall under the train and that she committed suicide. In her file on Charles Omerton, Martha McGillivray had noted that his mother had been a teacher and put a question mark against it, but stupidly I didn't check in what subject. It was chemistry. DC Sutton is probably going to unearth evidence of the purchase of a castor oil plant, but I don't think we need that for the coroner to come to the same conclusion."

"Will Hall and Smith keep their inheritance then?" Calderwood asked.

"I don't see why not," McCord replied. "The solicitor said the old signed will is the one that counts."

Calderwood nodded. "But why did McGillivray want to cut Hall out of her will? I can understand that she was disillusioned with her relationship with Smith, but what had Hall done to her?"

McCord sighed.

"I don't know what she was thinking but my guess is that McGillivray had become increasingly frustrated with her life, which she perceived as boring and insignificant. She began to suspect conspiracies wherever she went. When McGillivray took the photograph of Charles Omerton with the neo-Nazis, she expected Hall to do what McGillivray herself would have done: leave him and expose the threat to liberal society by members of the establishment cosying up to people trying to destroy it. Hall, however, was convinced that Charles Omerton's account of the meeting was true and refused, so McGillivray felt betrayed by her former protégée and friend. That's why she asked for her flat key back at the SKYbar."

Amy's thoughts had already moved on to the article for *Forth Write* which was forming in her head.

"Do you think Charles Omerton's career will survive having a murderer as a mother?"

McCord shrugged. "No idea. That probably depends on how the press decide to deal with him. To be honest, I don't give a damn either way."

At that very moment, there was a perfunctory knock on the door which swung open to reveal Superintendent Gilchrist, resplendent in his dress kilt but with a face that bode no good tidings.

McCord shot a glance at the door that concealed Amy from Gilchrist's view. He swiftly rose from his chair and moved towards his boss to discourage him from coming further into the office.

"Good evening, sir. I have already sent you my report about this evening's incident at Waverley."

"I've come straight from the Police Federation's Annual Dinner," Gilchrist said as if the poor timing of Sandra Omerton's death was McCord's fault. "Have you seen tomorrow's newspaper headlines?"

McCord was momentarily stunned into silence. "I've been rather busy dealing with an attempted murder and a suicide... sir."

The brief, insolent pause before the 'sir' was not lost on Gilchrist who now looked close to apoplexy.

"Exactly! An attempted murder of another journalist, and a pregnant one to boot, *and* a suicide, while two of my police officers are standing right next to them!"

McCord opened his mouth to protest but Gilchrist was not finished.

"And all of this would not have happened at all if the investigation into Martha McGillivray had been conducted more competently. That's what the papers are going to say, tomorrow, DI McCord, and it is not only your competence that is drawn into question but also mine as your superior officer! This is an absolute PR disaster!"

"Maybe I can help you with that, Superintendent," Amy said, stepping out from behind the door.

Gilchrist's eyes swivelled between Amy and McCord, his expression changing from surprise to embarrassment to anger and finally to suspicion.

"May I ask why you are here, Miss Thornton?" His voice changed from outrage at his orders being disobeyed to the unctuous tone he employed with members of the press.

Amy smiled calmly.

"The first reason why I'm here is that I am a material witness to the tragic events this evening, having been only a few yards away when they happened. I can swear to the fact that without DI McCord's dedication to the case, even during his very limited time off, and DC Calderwood's brave intervention, there would now not be the remains of a cold-blooded killer on the tracks of Waverley station but those of a murdered pregnant journalist."

Gilchrist shuddered involuntarily.

Amy pointed at the two detectives. "Your two officers not only solved an incredibly complex case today but also saved an innocent woman and her unborn child. And that is not all. During my own extensive investigation, which I conducted without any assistance from the police, as you well know..." – Amy paused to watch Gilchrist squirm – "DI McCord and DC Calderwood saved me from being raped and murdered."

Amy paused to let this sink in.

"The second reason I am here, Superintendent, is to gain some procedural detail from DI McCord and DC Calderwood for the extensive feature I was going to write in *Forth Write* magazine about the sterling job that you and your officers have been doing. But if you'd rather I didn't..."

"Good God, no," Gilchrist replied, spreading his arms wide. "If that's the case, I am sure that DI McCord and DC Calderwood, two of my best officers, as you know, will give you every assistance you require."

Gilchrist pulled himself up, every inch the commanding officer, and raised his eyebrows at McCord and Calderwood.

"Is that understood?"

"Yes, sir," McCord and Calderwood replied in unison.

Amy smiled sweetly.

"Thank you very much, Superintendent."

"And in future, Miss Thornton, as long as the correct procedures are followed, Police Scotland, and I personally, will be grateful for any positive input from a valued member of the press to assist us in our inquiries."

Amy bowed her head in acknowledgement.

"Of course, Superintendent. Would you mind if I took a picture of you to accompany my article?"

"Not at all, not at all." Gilchrist posed in front of the bare wall and put on his best PR smile.

Amy took a few pictures. "Thank you, Superintendent."

"You are most welcome. After all, it is vital that the general public gets a fair and honest assessment of how we carry out our duty of protecting the citizens of Edinburgh."

Seeming very pleased with himself, Gilchrist wished them all a good evening and withdrew.

When the door had closed behind him, Amy and Calderwood put their hands over their mouths to stifle the laughter that was bubbling up within them. McCord looked as if he could not quite believe the exchange that had taken place.

"You're a devious little genius, Amy," McCord said. "You've just saved me from another infernal course and got yourself back into the Super's good books."

He checked his phone.

"Damn. Is that the time? I need to apologise to John and your mum for ruining their evening."

"No need," Amy said. "I've already told them why we had to leave in such a hurry and everything that happened. You are forgiven. Mum even said you are a very clever man and a great detective."

"A notion of which you swiftly disengaged her, no doubt."

Amy shook her head.

"Sometimes, DI McCord, you are very slow on the uptake."

"Which I happily admit," he said.

Amy realised that he had misunderstood her, yet again, but it had been a long day.

She took both men's arms, McCord on her right, Calderwood on the left.

"Come on, both of you, let's find a bar that's still open. We all need a drink."

Without letting go of Amy's arm, McCord grabbed his coat.

"As long as it's not champagne!"

List of characters

Police

Superintendent Arthur Gilchrist
Detective Inspector Russell McCord
Detective Constable Duncan Calderwood
DC Heather 'The Hacker' Sutton
PC Mike Turner
PC Surina Dharwan
Jack Carruthers – Duty Sergeant
Dr Cyril Crane – pathologist

Others

Amy Thornton – journalist with *Forth Write* magazine
Martha McGillivray – freelance investigative journalist
(victim)
John Campbell – owner and editor of *Forth Write*
magazine
Martin Eden – political editor of *Forth Write* magazine
Dougal Johnstone – editor of *Edinburgh Messenger*
Kirsty Hall – journalist at *Edinburgh Messenger*
Cameron Coates – journalist at *Edinburgh Messenger*
Zane Smith – partner of Martha McGillivray
Shug McCain – ex-husband of Martha McGillivray
Godfrey Lomax – owner and CEO of Lomax Construction
Samantha Lomax – wife of Godfrey Lomax
Suzie – secretary to Godfrey Lomax

Councillor Weatherspoon – member of Borders Region Planning Committee
Charles Omerton – MSP for North Fife
Sandra Omerton – mother of Charles Omerton
Hector Billington – headmaster of St Nicodemus Academy
Mr & Mrs Bottomley – neighbours of Martha McGillivray
Keith McCord – father of DI Russell McCord
Clare Hildreth – owner of jewellery shop in Niddrie
Valerie Thornton – mother of Amy Thornton
Professor Thurrock – member of the Edinburgh Archaeological Field Society
Matt Branston – archaeologist
John Blackford – Martha McGillivray's solicitor
Drummond Wilson – Environmental Impact Assessor
Hamish Gillespie – farmer
Brodie Simpson – winner of Young Conservative Award

If you enjoyed this book, please let others know by leaving a quick review on Amazon. Also, if you spot anything untoward in the paperback, get in touch. We strive for the best quality and appreciate reader feedback.

editor@thebookfolks.com

Also in this series

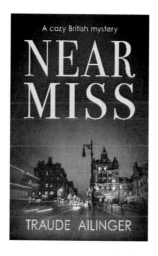

NEAR MISS (book 1)

After being nearly hit by a car, fashion journalist Amy
Thornton decides to visit the driver, who ends up in
hospital after evading her. Curious about this strange
man she becomes convinced she's unveiled a murder
plot. But it won't be so easy to persuade Scottish
detective DI Russell McCord.

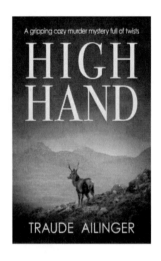

A gripping cozy murder mystery full of twists

HIGH HAND

TRAUDE AILINGER

HIGH HAND (book 2)

When a man is killed after a shooting party on a Scottish country estate, DI McCord gets nowhere interviewing the arrogant landowners. He'll have to rely on information passed on by journalist Amy Thornton, who is more accustomed to high society. But will his class resentment colour his judgement when it comes to putting the murderer behind bars?

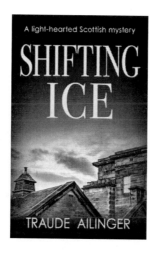

SHIFTING ICE (book 4)

After a jewellery thief meets a bitter end, DI McCord
tries to make sense of his dying words. Are they a clue
to his killer? He'll find out. Meanwhile journalist Amy
Thornton is forbidden from taking on dangerous
investigations, and sent on a fool's errand. Hmmm.
She'll wiggle out of just about anything. Except perhaps
the place she might hold in the cop's heart.

Other titles of interest

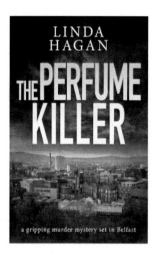

THE PERFUME KILLER by Linda Hagan

Stumped in a multiple murder investigation, with the only clue being a perfume bottle top left at a crime scene, DCI Gawn Girvin must wait for a serial killer to make a wrong move. Unless she puts herself in the firing line.

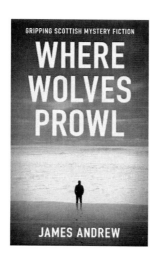

WHERE WOLVES PROWL by James Andrew

When loner Jason is invited by an attractive girl to a
luxury private pool party on Nairn's seafront, he can't
quite believe his luck. But when he learns the next day
that someone was murdered during the event, things
take a turn for the worse. As an outsider, he falls under
suspicion. Can he find out who the killer is and prove his
innocence?

Sign up to our mailing list to find out about new releases and special offers!

www.thebookfolks.com

Made in United States
North Haven, CT
21 September 2023

41819372R00143